m W P.S.

D0253533

Cate had a way ... seemed to like and trust her.

And she certainly knew how to keep them entertained. If they could work out an arrangement, he would be forever in his pastor's debt.

Though he knew little about Cate, he felt comfortable in her presence. Reassured, somehow, that things would work out. He found her as appealing as his niece and nephew did—on many levels, he realized, watching her blond hair brush her cheek.

When Cate turned toward him, her slight blush told him she was aware he'd been staring. Not good. He needed her child-care services. Making her nervous was not part of the plan.

"What are your plans for them?" Cate asked Clay.

"I don't know. I've been on my own for too many years. I never wanted a responsibility like this. But I made a promise to my sister. As long as the kids are with me, I want to do my best. But I can't do it alone. I need your help."

Books by Irene Hannon

Love Inspired

*Home for the Holidays
*A Groom of Her Own
*A Family to Call Her Own
It Had to Be You
One Special Christmas
The Way Home
Never Say Goodbye
Crossroads

**The Best Gift
**Gift from the Heart
**The Unexpected Gift
All Our Tomorrows
The Family Man
Rainbow's End
†From This Day Forward
†A Dream To Share
†Where Love Abides
Apprentice Father

*Vows
**Sisters & Brides
†Heartland Homecomings

IRENE HANNON

who writes both romance and romantic suspense, is the author of more than twenty-five novels. Her books have been honored with both the coveted RITA® Award from Romance Writers of America (the "Oscar" of romantic fiction) and the Reviewer's Choice Award from *Romantic Times BOOKreviews* magazine. More than one million copies of her novels have been sold worldwide. A former corporate communications executive with a Fortune 500 company, Irene now writes full-time. In her spare time, she enjoys singing, long walks, cooking, gardening and spending time with family. She and her husband make their home in Missouri. For more information about her and her books, Irene invites you to visit her Web site at www.irenehannon.com.

Apprentice Father
Irene Hannon

Steeple
Hill®

Published by Steeple Hill Books™

STEEPLE HILL BOOKS

Steeple
Hill®

Recycling programs
for this product may
not exist in your area.

ISBN-13: 978-0-373-87515-3
ISBN-10:   0-373-87515-0

APPRENTICE FATHER

Copyright © 2009 by Irene Hannon

www.SteepleHill.com

Printed in U.S.A.

God gives a home to the forsaken.
—Psalms 68:6

To my husband, Tom—
With love and gratitude for all you do…
and all you are

Prologue

The jarring ring of the phone slowly penetrated Clay's sleep-fogged brain. Groping for it in the dark, he squinted at his digital clock, trying to focus on the blue numbers. Three o'clock in the morning. Not good.

"Hello?" he mumbled.

"Clay Adams?"

"Yes."

"This is Lieutenant Butler with the Omaha, Nebraska, Police Department. You have a sister, Anne Montgomery?"

A surge of adrenaline shot through Clay and he jerked upright, his hand tightening on the phone as he swung his legs to the floor. "Yes."

"I'm very sorry to inform you that she was fatally injured tonight in a domestic violence incident."

Clay heard the words. Tried to process them. Couldn't. He'd talked to Anne just three days ago, when she'd called to tell him she was finally leaving her abusive husband. Tomorrow after work, he was making the drive from Washington, Missouri, to Omaha to pick up her and the kids.

She couldn't be dead.

"Sir?"

"Yes." Clay cleared his throat. "I'm here."

"I'm sorry to give you such bad news. We notified a Clayton Adams in Iowa as well. However, he's ill and unable to assist with any arrangements."

His father's illness was news to Clay. But he didn't keep in touch with his holier-than-thou old man. And he couldn't care less what his physical condition was. Thanks to the pressure he'd exerted, Anne had stayed in a dangerous marriage.

Now she was dead.

As the full impact of the officer's news began to sink in, a wave of nausea swept over Clay. He squeezed his eyes shut, as if that would somehow obliterate the reality. But it couldn't alter the facts. Anne was gone.

"What happened?" He managed to choke out the hoarse question.

The sound of shuffling papers came over the line. "According to the report, it appears she died from a blow to the head. The autopsy will confirm that."

All at once, Clay's shock gave way to rage. A rage that went at light speed from simmering to boiling. "I hope you lock up that monster and throw away the key," he spat out.

"Unfortunately, the suspect had disappeared by the time we arrived."

A muscle in Clay's jaw clenched. "You mean he's gone?"

"For the moment. But we'll find him. He took the family's car, and we've issued a BOLO alert on him."

"Did Anne report this before she…before she died?"

"No. From what we've been able to gather, the suspect locked the children in a bedroom when the dispute began. One of them climbed out a window and ran next door for help. The neighbors called the police."

Clay hadn't even thought about Josh and Emily. "Are the kids okay?"

"Physically, yes. But as you might expect, they're pretty traumatized. A friend of Mrs. Montgomery's is watching them until family arrives."

Meaning him. There was no one else.

Wiping a hand down his face, Clay tried to think. The construction project he'd been sent to Washington to oversee was in the critical start-up phase, and a late February snow had already put them behind schedule in the two weeks he'd been on site. His boss in Chicago wouldn't be too thrilled about his taking time off. But that was tough.

He glanced again at the clock. "I can be there by noon tomorrow."

"I'll pass that on to Mrs. Montgomery's friend. Let me give you her name and address."

Flipping on the light, Clay fumbled in the drawer of his nightstand for a pencil and paper. He jotted down the information in a script so shaky he hoped he'd be able to read it later.

"And give us a call once you arrive," the lieutenant finished. "We'll need you to fill out some paperwork. Is there anything else we can do for you in the meantime?"

"Find my sister's husband."

"We intend to. And if it's any comfort, your sister's friend told us she would notify their pastor, and that all of you would be remembered in the prayers of her congregation."

With an effort, Clay bit back the disparaging comment that sprang to his lips. Instead, he thanked the officer and hung up.

Clasping his shaky hands, he leaned forward and took several long, slow breaths as the lieutenant's last comment echoed in his mind. He'd grown up in a so-called Christian home. A house-hold where the slightest transgression was punished. Where hell and damnation were preached, and guilt was ladled out in generous portions. Where the God of vengeance and punish-ment held court, and where unrepentant sinners—like him—were dealt with harshly and told to pray for mercy.

Back then, Clay hadn't thought much of prayer. He thought even less of it now, the taste of bitterness sharp on his tongue. Anne had prayed. But where had God been when she'd needed Him a few hours ago? And what good were the prayers of her congregation now? Anne was gone, leaving a four- and five-year-old motherless.

As for him…he didn't need God's help. He'd learned long ago to take care of himself.

Of course, if God wanted to lend a hand, that was fine. He was going to need all the help he could get in the days to come.

But he sure wasn't going to count on it.

Chapter One

As the service for Anne droned on, Clay checked on the two children sitting beside him, who were huddled close together in the pew, holding hands. Emily's long, dark hair was pulled back with a ribbon, and her eyes were huge in her pale face. Fair-haired Josh looked uncertain and lost, his freckles standing in stark relief against his pale skin, one finger stuck in his mouth. He hadn't said a word since Clay had arrived in Omaha.

Redirecting his attention to the sanctuary, where Reverend Phelps was presiding over Anne's funeral, Clay tried not to appear too hostile. He hadn't been inside a church since his sister's wedding almost ten years ago, and he'd prefer not to be in one now. But Anne would have wanted a church service. That's why he'd thrown his one suit into his suitcase in the early morning hours preceding his long, solitary drive to Nebraska.

He'd always been a sucker about giving his gentle, loving kid sister what she wanted, he recalled. His favorite comic book, his last piece of chocolate. He'd been her biggest fan when she'd had the leading role in her grade school play, and her staunchest defender when bullies had plagued her in middle school.

Yet he hadn't been able to save her from the ultimate bully. From the man who, ironically, had pledged to love, honor and cherish her all the days of his life.

As he looked at the coffin resting beside him in the aisle, Clay's throat tightened. A tear leaked out the corner of his eye, and he dipped his head to swipe at it with the back of his hand.

May Martin rot in hell for all eternity, Clay thought, the bitter wish twisting his gut.

And his feelings toward his old man weren't much kinder.

Nor were they tempered by the memory of their brief conversation after he'd arrived in Nebraska. He hadn't seen or talked with his father since Anne's wedding, and he hadn't recognized the querulous voice on the phone. But though his father had sounded old and feeble, he'd been as self-righteous, demanding—and disapproving—as ever.

"Listen, boy, I can't make it to Nebraska for the service. I have pneumonia." His father's hacking cough, followed by audible wheezing, had interrupted their conversation. "You'll have to handle the arrangements."

Clay had always hated how his father called him "boy." His jaw had clamped shut and he'd gritted his teeth. "I plan to."

"There has to be a church service."

"It's taken care of."

"Who has the children?"

"I do."

"I guess there's no other option right now."

He must think I'll corrupt them in a week, Clay had concluded, compressing his mouth into a thin line.

"I'll take them as soon as I'm well enough," his father had continued. "I'll call you."

And with that he'd hung up.

There hadn't been a lot of opportunity to think about his father's last comment, but as the organ launched into a hymn and the people around him began to sing, Clay considered the two children beside him. He'd been so mired in grief, so bogged down in paperwork and funeral arrangements, he hadn't given much thought to their future.

But as he regarded their innocent, anxious faces, his heart contracted with compassion. How could he relegate these little children to a cold, joyless life with his strict, hard-nosed father? After the trauma they'd been through, they needed love and tenderness, and a stable, supportive environment. They needed a caring parent figure and a real home. His father would offer none of those things.

Unfortunately, he wasn't equipped to offer them, either, Clay acknowledged. He didn't know much about love or tenderness, and less about how to create a comforting haven. The home of his youth wasn't a good prototype. Nor were his twelve years in the Army, where the focus had been on structure and discipline and honor. And his current job kept him on the move, making it impossible to establish ties of any kind—or even a permanent home. And that's the way he liked it.

Yet the thought of handing these children over to his father turned his stomach. The old man ruled through fear, not love. *Joy* and *fun* weren't in his vocabulary. Josh and Emily would have a dismal life with him. That was the last thing Anne would have wanted for them.

So what was he supposed to do?

"As we take our sister, Anne, to her final resting place, let us find some comfort in knowing she is at peace and with God." Reverend Phelps's closing remarks echoed in the church, and Clay tried to focus on his words. "And let us recall how she always tried to do the right thing. That's a challenge we all face. Because the right thing may not always be the easiest thing. It may not be what we want to do. It may take great courage. But Anne gave us a shining example of courage and selfless love. Let that be her legacy to us, one that we all strive to follow."

Twin furrows dented Clay's brow. He'd seen too many people fail at relationships—with parents, with spouses, with children. Enough to convince him he never wanted a family. But if what the minister said was true, he had one now. For how could he send these children to his father's home, where their life would be little better than before?

All at once Clay found it difficult to breathe. Reaching up, he tugged at his suddenly too-tight tie. He'd had this feeling of being trapped, of the walls closing in on him, twice before in his life. Once, as a kid, living under his father's roof. And again, during Army training, when he'd been locked into a small, dark room for several days during a POW simulation. In both cases, he'd survived for one simple reason: he'd known he would get out.

But there was no escape from this situation. Not if he did the right thing.

Clay knew about duty from his years in the military. Knew about it, too, from years of living in his father's house, where the phrase "doing your Christian duty" had been drummed into him. The minister had confirmed that obligation. There was no doubt in Clay's mind about what he *should* do.

But he wasn't sure he was up to the task.

Frustrated, Clay raked his fingers through his hair. He didn't know a thing about little kids. If Anne had listened to him and left her husband instead of letting their father shame her into staying in that mockery of a marriage, he wouldn't be in this predicament.

Giving him yet another reason to resent his old man.

As the pallbearers began to roll the coffin out, Clay moved into the aisle behind it. Emily and Josh remained in the pew, watching him with big eyes. He motioned for them to follow, and Emily nudged Josh. But the little boy shook his head and burrowed closer to Emily.

Stepping back into the pew, Clay crouched beside the children. "It's time to go," he murmured.

"Josh is 'fraid," Emily whispered.

A lump rose in this throat. "Neither of you need to be afraid anymore. I'm going to take care of you. How about I carry you, Josh? That way, you can see the pretty windows in the back."

Clay held out his arms and, with a nudge from Emily, Josh edged toward him. Swinging him up, Clay was startled by how little the boy weighed—and reminded yet again of the children's vulnerability…and the terrifying responsibility he'd inherited.

As the procession moved down the aisle, a tentative touch on his hand drew his attention and he looked down. Emily was watching him, her expression uncertain, as if to ask: *Is this okay?* In response, he pasted on a smile and folded her small, cold hand in his with a gentle squeeze.

The tremulous little puff of air she released, the sudden relaxing of her features, almost undid him. Clay knew Anne had tried her very best to shelter her children and create a real home. But in the few days he'd been in Nebraska, he'd discovered her best hadn't been good enough. The children had seen too much. Heard too much. Their eyes told the story. Fearful, anxious, uncertain, haunted—they were old beyond their years. Especially Emily's. The damage was clear. And he was afraid it would take a miracle to undo it.

Clay didn't much believe in miracles…except the kind people made for themselves through hard work and perseverance. In this case, however, he wasn't sure any amount of work on his part would give these children back their childhood. Yet they were in desperate need of help.

Since he doubted he'd darken a church door again any time soon, Clay figured he should use this opportunity to seek help from a higher source. Not that he expected much. But what did he have to lose?

God, I don't know why any of this happened. And I don't know if You care. But if You do, please take pity on these children. They need more than I can give. I'll do my best, but I'm not equipped to handle kids. If You're listening, help me find a way to heal these children. Not for my sake. But for theirs. And Anne's.

Clay saw the familiar arches in the distance, a short drive off the interstate, and cast an uneasy glance into the rearview mirror as he pulled into the exit lane. Josh was dozing in the back seat, and Emily was staring out the window. Since leaving Omaha four hours ago after the funeral, she hadn't said more than ten words. And the eerie silence was beginning to unnerve him. Weren't kids supposed to be noisy and restless on long car trips? Weren't they supposed to chatter and ask how much longer and want a drink of water and need to use the bathroom every ten miles?

These two, however, hadn't made one request or asked a single question during the entire trip. But they must be hungry by now. He sure was.

"How about some hamburgers and French fries?" Clay tossed the question over his shoulder as he started up the exit ramp.

No response.

He checked the rearview mirror again. Emily's somber gaze met his.

"Are you hungry?" He gentled his tone.

She gave a slow nod.

"Do you like hamburgers and French fries?"

Again, an affirmative response. "Josh does, too."

"How about a milkshake to go with them?"

Her face lit up a little and she gave her brother a gentle prod. "Josh. Wake up. We're going to have milkshakes." It was the first touch of life Clay had heard in her voice.

A parking spot near the front door of the fast-food outlet opened up, and Clay pulled in. By the time he climbed out of the pickup truck, Emily had unbuckled her car seat and was working on Josh's, her lower lip caught between her teeth.

"Do you need some help?" Clay offered.

"No, thank you. I can do it."

Five minutes later, after he'd settled them in a booth, Clay headed for the counter to place his order, keeping them in sight. But he didn't have to worry. Unlike the other children in the place, who were crying, shouting, throwing food or running around, Josh and Emily sat in silence waiting for him. While Clay wasn't anxious for them to emulate their peers, he was struck again by the need to restore some semblance of childhood to their lives. Some laughter and spontaneity and just plain silliness.

In light of all that had transpired, however, that seemed like a monumental task.

"Here's your change, sir."

Clay swiveled toward the counter and pocketed the money. "Thanks." Juggling the tray, he wove his way toward the booth, slid in opposite the children and quickly dispensed the food.

The first bite of his burger was wonderful, and he closed his eyes as he chewed, enjoying the flavor. At least, he *was* enjoying it until he opened his eyes and found Josh and Emily staring at him with solemn faces, their food untouched.

He stopped chewing. "What's wrong?"

"We didn't say grace yet," Emily said.

Trying not to choke, Clay swallowed his mouthful of burger with a gulp and wiped a paper napkin across his lips. He hadn't said a prayer before meals since he'd left home at age seventeen. Racking his brain, he searched for the stale words his father used to say, but they eluded him.

Emily studied him. "Do you want me to say it?"

"Good idea," he endorsed with relief.

She reached for Josh's hand, then for his. Josh inched his other hand across the table, and Clay took it. Their small hands were swallowed in his much larger grasp.

Emily and Josh bowed their heads as Emily spoke. "Lord, thank you for this food we eat, and keep us safe until we meet. Amen."

"Amen," Clay echoed after they gave him an expectant look.

As the children began eating, devouring every last morsel, Clay realized how hungry they'd been. And how dependent they were on him. For everything. Food. Shelter. Security. Love. Like it or not, he'd inherited a family. Unless he sent them to live with his father.

That was still an option. But not a good one.

Meaning his life was about to change dramatically.

And all at once he wasn't hungry any more.

"Don't make any noise, Josh."

The childish, high-pitched whisper penetrated Clay's light sleep, and he squinted at the illuminated dial of his watch. Four-fifteen. If he didn't get some rest soon, he'd be a zombie in the morning. But the uncomfortable couch that had become his bed since Emily and Josh had claimed his room three nights ago wasn't helping, either.

An odd sound came from the bedroom, and he frowned. What was going on in there?

Swinging his legs to the floor, Clay padded toward the bedroom door, his bare feet noiseless on the carpet. As he eased it open, two heads pivoted toward him and Josh and Emily froze, like startled deer caught in headlights.

The seconds ticked by as Clay tried to make sense of the scene. The two children stood at the far corner of the bed. Emily had taken the blankets off and piled them on the floor. Now she was trying to take the sheets off as well.

"What's going on?" Clay scanned the room again, bewildered.

Josh moved closer to Emily, and she placed a shielding arm around his shoulders. "Josh h-had an accident."

Shifting his attention to the frightened little boy, Clay gave him a rapid inspection. In his definition, "accidents" entailed injury and blood. But Josh didn't appear to be hurt. However, his pajama bottoms did look funny. They were clinging to him. Like they were wet.

All at once, Clay understood.

"It happens s-sometimes at night, if he's afraid." A tremor ran through Emily's voice. "I can clean it up. You don't have t-to be mad."

Clay took a step into the room—but came to an abrupt halt when Josh cowered behind Emily with a whimper.

They were scared. Really scared, he realized with a jolt. Anne had said that Martin had never hurt them, but now he wasn't sure that was true. Softening his tone, he moved slowly into the room. "Accidents happen. It's okay. Emily, why don't you help Josh change into dry pajamas while I put new sheets on the bed?"

She took her brother's hand and tugged. "Come on, Josh."

The little boy followed, skirting him warily.

After scrubbing and blow-drying the mattress, remaking the bed and tucking a folded towel under the fitted sheet on Josh's side, Clay beckoned the children. "Okay. Good as new. Climb in."

Emily got in first, then pulled Josh up beside her. She pressed him down on the pillow and lay next to him, taking his hand. Clay tucked the blanket under their chins and sat on the edge of the bed.

"I know everything is new, and that you miss your mommy. But I'll take care of you. You don't need to be scared."

"How come you didn't get mad at Josh?" Emily searched his face.

"He didn't do it on purpose."

"I know. But Daddy always got mad."

With an effort, Clay kept his expression neutral and tried for a measured tone. "What did he do when he got mad?"

"He yelled at Josh. And at Mommy."

"Did he spank Josh?"

"No. But I think…I think he hit Mommy. He said it was her fault we had accidents. I spilled a glass of milk once, and Daddy yelled at Mommy. She had big bruises on her arm the next day." Emily's features contorted with misery. "We didn't m-mean to hurt Mommy." The last word caught on a sob. "We tried t-to be good."

Clay felt as if someone had punched him in the stomach. With an unsteady hand he brushed the hair back from his niece's forehead. It was soft and fine and gossamer.

"It wasn't your fault that your mommy got hurt, Emily. Or Josh's. Your daddy shouldn't have yelled at you about accidents, and he shouldn't have hurt your mommy. That was a wrong thing to do."

"I wish M-Mommy was here now."

"So do I." More than Emily would ever know, he reflected. "But she would want you to be brave. Will you try to do that?"

Emily gave a tearful nod and looked at Josh, who had fallen asleep again, cuddled up beside her. "Josh is kind of little to be brave, though."

Clay swallowed past the lump in his throat. "Then we'll have to help him."

"Okay." Emily snuggled next to Josh, and her eyelids drifted closed.

For several more minutes Clay sat there. Once their even breathing told him they were asleep he rose and headed toward the door, pausing on the threshold. The two youngsters were lost in the queen sized bed, their bodies an almost indiscernible bump beneath the blanket. They seemed so tiny. So forlorn. So defenseless. And they were relying on him to see to all of their needs.

Their physical needs, Clay could handle. Food, clothing and shelter weren't hard to provide.

But when it came to matters of the heart, he was in way over his head.

She was about to hear bad news.

Cate Shepard knew it the minute she walked in the back door of the Dugan home and found both Brenna and Steve waiting for her. In the two years she'd provided in-home child care for their son they'd become good friends, and she'd learned to read their moods.

"Good morning." She closed the door and summoned up a smile, steeling herself. "Why do I think this isn't my lucky day?"

Brenna sent a quick look to Steve, who cleared his throat and rose.

"It's one of those good news, bad news scenarios, Cate. I've been offered a great position with a new company in Chicago. Starting in two weeks. The bad news is we'll have to leave behind the best child care provider we'll ever hope to find."

She was out of a job.

Cate managed to keep her smile in place. This had happened before; it would happen again. She'd manage, as she always did.

"I'm happy for you, Steve. But I'll miss all of you."

"We feel the same way about you, Cate." Brenna stood and came forward to give her a hug. "You know we'll give you a stellar recommendation."

"Thank you." Cate gave her a squeeze, then stepped back. "Now tell me about the new opportunity."

She listened as the young couple explained Steve's new position, commiserated with Brenna about her angst over finding a new job, and took care of Timmy for the rest of the day when the couple went to work.

Only later, as she drove through the streets of Washington to her condo—with a quick detour for a fudgesicle at a convenience store—did she let herself think about the future.

She always hated her jobs to end. In ten years of providing on-site child care, she'd been lucky to go through this only three times. Now she had to start the process over again. And while she'd never had trouble connecting with a family in need of her services, she usually had far more notice than this to find a new position.

Pulling into the parking place near her condo, she picked up the fudgesicle. It was already softening in the unseasonable warmth of this early March Missouri day, she noted, walking to her front door as fast as her slightly uneven gait allowed.

Once inside, she headed for the kitchen and unwrapped the treat. Leaning over the sink while she ate, she savored the fleeting sweetness as the rich chocolate melted on her tongue. And recalled, as she always did, the day she'd indulged in one after receiving the letter that had offered her a bright and shining future.

But two weeks later, that future had melted away, as surely and irrevocably as her dissolving fudgesicle.

Rinsing her sticky hands under the sink, her gaze lingered on the fingers of her left hand as a melancholy pang echoed through her. Long, slender and graceful, they looked the same as they always had. They just didn't work as well.

Yet dwelling on memories of a time when hopes were high and dreams came true was fruitless, she reminded herself. Her life was good now. She had a satisfying career. A loving family. A solid faith that had seen her through some rough stretches. If she didn't have the one thing she most yearned for—a loving marriage blessed with children—she needed to accept that it wasn't in God's plan for her. And she was working on it.

But it wasn't easy.

Securing the pillow under his head with a firm shove, Clay fought off consciousness—and reality—as long as possible. A week and a half into his new role as surrogate father, he was sinking fast.

The kids had been thrown out of day care on Friday because four-year-old bed wetters weren't acceptable, so he had to come up with alternative arrangements by tomorrow. And he had a ton of work to do that he hadn't gotten to last week, thanks to all the changes in his life.

It was not shaping up to a be a good Sunday.

And the sober faces peering at him when he finally pried open his eyes suggested it was only going to get worse. Emily and Josh were already dressed, he noted. In nice clothes.

"It's Sunday." The pronouncement came from Emily.

She said that like it was supposed to mean something. And Clay had the distinct impression that it did not include sleeping in.

"I know." He hoped she wasn't heading in the direction he suspected.

"Aren't we going to church?"

His hope dissolved. "Maybe we could skip this week."

Tears pooled in Emily's eyes. "Mommy told us once that if she ever went away to be with God, we could talk to her in church on Sunday."

Clay was sunk. He could hold his own with hard-as-nails, give-no-quarter types. But these two little kids, who together couldn't weigh much more than sixty pounds, melted his heart. Meaning his Sundays were about to undergo a radical change.

Forty-five minutes later, as he approached the white church with the tall steeple that he passed on the way to work everyday, he hoped the lot would be empty. That way, he could rationalize that he'd *tried* to take the kids to church.

But no, it was full. And he could hear the muffled sound of organ music. According to the sign in front, the service had begun ten minutes ago.

He was stuck.

Accepting his fate, he helped the children out of the truck, took their hands and headed toward a church for the second time in less than a week. Although he tried to unobtrusively slip into a row near the back, Josh foiled his plan by tripping over the edge of the pew and sprawling in the aisle. Clay was sure every head in the place swiveled their direction as he swooped to pick up the little boy.

After climbing over three sets of feet and squeezing in between a woman with two teenagers and an older couple, all Clay wanted to do was slink out of the church and never come near the place again.

The kids, however, were oblivious to his embarrassment. Emily's hands lay folded in her lap, and Josh was jiggling his feet, which stuck straight out over the end of the pew. Noting that one of the youngster's shoes was untied, Clay leaned forward to remedy the situation—and discovered another problem he couldn't fix. Josh's socks didn't match.

Risking a peek at the older woman beside him, he saw her inspecting Josh's feet. A flush crawled up his neck. The fact that it had never occurred to him to check the kids' clothes was yet more evidence of how ill-equipped he was for this job.

The woman lifted her head, and Clay braced for disapproval. Instead he saw understanding and compassion in her eyes.

"Kids are a handful, aren't they?" The whispered comment was accompanied by a smile. "I had four. And I had that same problem on a few occasions." She inclined her head toward Josh's feet.

Relief coursed through him. The woman wasn't judging him. She wasn't trying to make him feel inadequate. She was being kind. He hadn't expected that.

"I'm pretty new at this. I have a lot to learn."

"Don't we all," she commiserated with a quiet chuckle before turning her attention back to the sanctuary, where the minister was moving toward the pulpit.

Clay's tension eased. Most of the Christians he recalled from his childhood had been quick to criticize and censure. But this woman hadn't done that. Nor had the members of Anne's congregation. It was a new view of Christianity for Clay.

This minister was also worth listening to. Mid-forties, with flecks of silver in his light brown hair and subtle character lines in his face, he spoke in a down-to-earth style, and his words had practical implications. Though Clay hadn't picked up a Bible in decades, the passage the pastor referenced near the end of his sermon was vaguely familiar. But he'd never looked at it in quite the way that the minister presented it.

"I'm sure most of you know the story about the fig tree that didn't bear fruit," he said. "The frustrated owner planned to cut it down, but the vine dresser entreated him to give the vine one more chance.

"How often in our lives have we, too, wanted one more chance? One more chance to say I love you. To prove our abilities. To do the right thing. One more chance to be the person God intended us to be. Sad to say, those feelings often surface at funerals and on death beds—when it's too late to change things."

The minister leaned forward and gripped the pulpit. "My dear friends, God doesn't want us to have regrets. Like the vine dresser, He offers us countless opportunities to put things right. In fact, each day that He gives us is one more chance—to mend a relationship, to lend a helping hand, to welcome Him into our lives with open hearts and minds. Let us take comfort in knowing He is always there to guide us, to console us, to strengthen us. To give us one more chance."

As the minister concluded his remarks, Clay looked over at the two children beside him. Was he the one who was supposed to give them the chance the minister had talked about?

It was a daunting thought.

Even more daunting was the thought that came next; maybe they had been brought into his life to give *him* one more chance, too.

Now that was a scary concept. It reeked too much of commitment. Of long-term responsibility. The very things he'd spent a lifetime trying to avoid. He'd seen how much damage people could inflict on those they claimed to love, and he'd decided long ago that love wasn't worth the risk. Besides, the demands of his job weren't conducive to having a family. Nor were they compatible with single parenthood. Surely no one would expect him to change his whole life for two little kids who weren't even his own. Would they?

Maybe.

The answer came unbidden—and unwanted. Prompted, he supposed, by the lack of other options. For if he sent the kids to live with his father, they would never have the chance to lead a normal life.

Tension began to form behind Clay's temples. He didn't normally get headaches. But the last ten days hadn't been anywhere close to normal. And the organist, who seemed intent on banging his or her way through the final hymn at the highest possible volume, wasn't helping.

When the last note mercifully died away, Clay leaned down to guide the children out of the pew. As he did so, the older woman touched his arm.

"They're darling children. So well behaved. Good luck with them."

Clay acknowledged the woman's encouraging words with a nod. But they didn't begin to solve his child care problem.

As they inched toward the exit, the children's hands tucked in his, it occurred to Clay that the woman might have some suggestions on child care. His step faltered and he turned to scan the crowd, but she'd already disappeared. Too bad. He could have used one more chance with her, he mused, recalling the minister's sermon.

The minister.

Perhaps the preacher might know of someone who could help with the children, Clay speculated. Clergy often had a network of social service resources. Plus, a minister would only recommend someone trustworthy and above reproach. That meant Clay wouldn't have to worry about checking references. It was worth trying, anyway.

Because he was out of options.

And he was running out of time.

Chapter Two

As he left the church, Clay spotted the pastor greeting members of the congregation. He stepped aside to wait until the man was free, watching as Emily dug in her pocket and withdrew a plastic bag of cereal.

"I brought these for Josh." She gave him an uncertain look. "Mommy always put some cereal in her purse for him in case he got hungry at church."

In the rush of getting them ready, he'd forgotten to feed them, Clay realized with a pang. "That was a good idea. I think we're all hungry. After I talk to the minister, why don't we go out to breakfast?"

"To a restaurant?" Emily's face lit up.

"Yes."

"Could we get pancakes?"

"Sure."

"We'd like that. Wouldn't we, Josh?"

The little boy looked up at Clay and gave a slow nod.

"It's a date, then," Clay promised.

The crowd around the minister began to disperse, and Clay

ushered the children in his direction. As they approached, the man gave them a pleasant smile. "Good morning. I'm Bob Richards. Welcome."

"Thank you. Clay Adams." He grasped the man's extended hand.

"I'm happy you could join us this morning." The pastor transferred his attention to Emily and Josh. "Can I meet these two lovely children?"

"This is my niece and nephew, Emily and Josh." Clay rested a hand on each of their shoulders. "They just lost their mother...my sister...so they've come to live with me."

"I'm very sorry." The man's quiet words were laced with empathy.

Clay acknowledged the expression of sympathy with a nod. "I'd like to ask your advice, if I may. I'm trying to find someone who can come to my apartment and watch the children while I'm at work, just until things settle down and I can make more permanent arrangements. I'm a construction engineer." He mentioned the manufacturing facility he'd been sent to build. "I'm new in town, and I thought you might be able to direct me to some resources."

The man's face grew thoughtful. "As a matter of fact, I know someone who's between child care jobs." He surveyed the people chatting in small groups. "Give me a minute."

He strode across the lawn, and Clay watched in surprise as he stopped beside a slender woman with blond hair. Her back was to him, but when the minister spoke to her she angled toward him, giving Clay a clear view of her profile. He'd expected the pastor to recommend someone older, not a beautiful young woman. But at this point, he'd hire anyone the man endorsed.

The woman's gaze skimmed his before she resumed her conversation with the minister. After a bit more discussion, they broke away from the group. Reverend Richards took her arm as they traversed the uneven ground, and Clay discovered the man's gesture was prompted by more than simple courtesy. The woman not only limped, she used a cane. Was she between jobs as the result of an injury? And with such a pronounced limp, how would she be able to keep up with two active children?

Despite his concern about her abilities, Clay was struck again by the woman's delicate beauty. From a distance, he'd guessed her to be in her early twenties. But as they drew close, he realized she was more likely in her thirties.

After performing the introductions, the minister excused himself. "I'll leave you two to discuss the details. But if there's anything else I can do, don't hesitate to call." He handed Clay a card. "And I hope to see you again soon at services."

"Thank you." Clay pocketed the card. "You've been very kind."

"It's in the job description. For all Christians—not just ministers." With a wink and a wave, the pastor headed toward another small cluster of congregants.

Cate watched him leave, then turned her attention to Clay. "I understand you're in need of child care on a temporary basis."

"Yes." He found himself admiring the way her soft hair framed the perfect oval of her face as well as her clear, emerald-green eyes. "My sister was…she recently passed away, and I'm caring for her children."

"Did you try the child care centers in town?"

"That didn't work out. I'd be happy to provide more details, but this may not be the best place." He gave a subtle nod toward Emily and Josh, who were watching the exchange with trepidation.

To his relief, she picked up his cue. "All right. But I'd like to meet the children." Bending down to their level, she braced herself on her cane and gave them a sunny smile. "Hi. I'm Cate. Can you tell me your names?"

Emily tightened her grip on Josh's hand. "I'm Emily. This is Josh."

"I'm very happy to meet you both."

"Did you hurt your leg?" Emily inspected the cane.

"Emily!" At Clay's sharp rebuke, the little girl flinched and shrank back.

Cate, however, took the question in stride. "I was sick a long time ago, and my leg never got all the way better. Neither did my hand."

As she lifted her left hand, Clay saw that it had limited function, too.

Casting an uncertain glance at Clay, Emily edged closer to Cate and lowered her voice. "Do they hurt?"

"Not too much anymore. Most days I don't need this." She indicated the cane. "But I was working in my garden on Friday, and I got a little sore."

"Mommy had a garden. With roses and 'tunias and ble-ble-gonias."

"Those are some of my favorites, too." She turned to Josh, her smile warm and open. "What's your favorite flower?"

As Josh studied Cate, he withdrew his thumb from his mouth. Clay signaled to her. "He doesn't…"

"Daisies," Josh interrupted.

Clay stared at him.

"I like those, too." Cate's smile deepened, and she took Josh's hand in a gentle clasp.

"We're having pancakes for breakfast. At a restaurant," he told her. "Can you come?"

"Not today. But I'll see you soon."

With a slight wince, she straightened up. "When would you like to get together?"

She directed her question to Clay, but he was still focused on Josh. The boy had spoken! It was a breakthrough.

Raising his head, Clay regarded Cate. Her physical limitations were obvious. Yet the minister had said she was between child care jobs, so she must be able to handle kids. She was sure handling Emily and Josh like a pro. If she could get Josh to talk, perhaps she could also help erase the haunted look from their eyes. "Would this afternoon be okay?"

"I'm sorry. I always have supper with my family on Sunday afternoon."

"I hate to impose." Clay tried not to appear too desperate. "But I'm overseeing a major construction project and I've already missed too much work. I need to get an arrangement in place as soon as possible."

For a terrifying instant Clay thought she was going to refuse. But to his relief, she relented.

"Okay. I can stop by before I go to supper." She withdrew a slip of paper and a pen from her purse. "What's your address and phone number?" She jotted it down as he dictated. "I'll come by about one, Mr. Adams."

"Make it Clay."

"And I'm Cate." She bent down to the children again. "I'll see you both later today."

"Promise?" Josh asked.

"Cross my heart." Smiling, she tousled his hair and stood to address Clay. "See you later."

"Thanks again."

As he watched her walk away, he found himself admiring her lithe figure. But beyond her loveliness, he'd been struck by how her mere presence had dissipated some of the turmoil that had clenched his stomach into knots since that fateful phone call ten days ago. With Cate in charge of the kids, he had a feeling he'd no longer feel as if his life was spinning out of control.

Taking the children's hands, he guided them back toward his truck. And made a reluctant admission.

Going to church today hadn't been a waste of time after all.

Cate double-checked the directions she'd printed from Mapquest. Two more turns and she should be at the apartment complex Clay Adams called home.

She still wasn't quite sure why she'd agreed to meet him today. She didn't believe in working on Sunday. But those two little children, with their big, solemn eyes, had touched her heart. They both needed a hefty dose of TLC.

Nor had she been immune to the desperation in their uncle's eyes.

But those weren't the only reasons she'd waived her no-work-on-Sunday rule, she acknowledged, as she negotiated the final turn before the entrance to his apartment complex. She'd also been drawn to the man himself.

Why, she wasn't sure. With his dark good looks, golden tan and slightly rough-around-the-edges demeanor, he was nothing like the boy-next-door type that usually appealed to her.

Perhaps his generosity had captured her fancy, she speculated as she pulled into a parking space close to Clay's apartment. Though grieving himself, he'd assumed responsibility for his sister's children. And his efforts to find quality care for them suggested he possessed a kind and caring heart. She admired him for that.

But that odd little flutter in her stomach when their gazes had met across the church grounds couldn't be explained away by mere admiration, she admitted. It had been attraction, pure and simple. Clay Adams might not be her type, but he was handsome in a rugged, bad-boy sort of way that for some reason made her heart race. She wasn't quite comfortable with the notion of working for someone to whom she was attracted. Yet for the sake of those two forlorn children, she could learn to control her reaction to him. She was sure of it.

After setting the brake, she inspected the apartment development. It was well-maintained and landscaped, but there was very little open green space, and no play area, she noted. At least there was a park not far away. If she accepted this job, Cate intended to take the children there often. Their wan appearance suggested they needed fresh air, along with a place to run and play and just be kids.

Opening her car door, Cate swung her legs to the ground and scooted to the edge of the seat. Although she hated to admit it, she'd overdone it in the garden a couple of days ago. Not only had she put extra strain on her leg, she'd pulled a muscle in her back.

Once on her feet, she reached for her cane. In a day or two, she should be able to put that nuisance back in the closet. For now, though, it was a godsend. Especially when she realized Clay's apartment was on the second floor. She could handle steps, but it was slow going even on a good day.

As if on cue, a door on the landing opened. She looked up to find her potential employer watching her.

"I forgot to tell you about the steps," he called down, his expression troubled.

She smiled. "No problem."

He hovered at the top, his concern obvious. It was a common reaction, and Cate was used to it. Many people were uncomfortable around those with disabilities, at least in the beginning. And sometimes forever. She'd been that way herself once, in the days when she'd moved with grace and perfect coordination. She understood his unease. She also knew that the best way to deal with it was to address it head-on.

"Can I help?" Clay offered.

"No, thanks. I'm fine. Just slow today."

Cate ascended the stairs, steadying herself on her cane once she reached the top. Much to her dismay, her stomach fluttered again as she looked into the intense, dark brown eyes that were fixed on her.

"Steps aren't always easy for me, but I'm very capable of handling the children," she assured him, striving for a confident tone. "You're seeing me at my worst, thanks to a gardening binge. Most of the time I don't use the cane. I've had years to learn how to manage my disability, and it's never hindered my work. Of course, your concern that Josh and Emily receive the best of care is commendable. I'll be happy to provide some references."

Warmth crept up Clay's neck. He considered himself to be a pretty tolerant and unbiased guy, but he didn't often come into contact with people who had physical disabilities. And despite the positive spin she'd given his obvious unease by praising his concern for the children's welfare, her graciousness didn't alleviate his chagrin.

"I'm sure Reverend Richards wouldn't have recommended you if you weren't capable."

"True. But it's best to get any reservations on the table at the beginning. I've learned that people are often curious about my disabilities, and I don't mind talking about them if that will help put your mind at ease."

He shoved his hands in his pockets and shifted his weight. He *was* curious. And not just because he was concerned about Cate's ability to deal with the children. She was a beautiful woman—and far too young to have to rely on a cane. He wanted to know what had happened to her.

"Fourteen years ago, when I was eighteen, I had Guillain-Barre Syndrome." She answered his question before he could figure out a diplomatic way to ask it. "Are you familiar with that condition?"

"I've heard the name. But that's all."

"You're not alone. Few people know much about it. It's a rare illness that generally affects men over the age of forty, so I wasn't a typical victim. It causes the body's immune system to attack the nerves. Most people make a full recovery."

She paused, and Clay saw a brief flash of pain ricochet across her eyes. "I take it you weren't typical in that regard, either."

"No. And since I didn't fit the standard profile, I wasn't diagnosed fast enough. I ended up paralyzed and went into respiratory failure. Even with symptoms that severe, however, most people recover. Longer-lasting effects, like lingering weakness in the arms or legs, usually go away with physical therapy. In a few cases, they don't."

Like hers.

The facts were clear, but there was much she hadn't spoken of, Clay reflected. And questions she hadn't answered. Like how had it felt, at the age of eighteen, to be struck with such a debilitating condition? How had it changed her life? What dreams had she been forced to give up? How had she found the strength to cope?

He couldn't begin to fathom what it must have been like for her to suddenly find her world so constricted, her options so limited.

"I'm sorry." It was a pathetically inadequate response, and he knew it

The door behind him creaked, and Clay swung around to find

Emily peering through the crack, reminding him that he should have invited Cate in instead of letting her tell her life story while standing on the landing.

His neck grew warm and he motioned toward the door. "Why don't we go inside?" Stepping aside to let her precede him, he was struck again by her delicate, willowy frame and her long, slender fingers as they gripped her cane.

For some reason, he was tempted to reach out, take her arm, reassure her, help her. It was an odd inclination—and completely inappropriate, he reminded himself, shoving his hands into the pockets of his jeans instead. She was here about a job. Nothing more.

"Hi, Cate," Emily greeted their visitor in a soft, shy voice.

"Hello, Emily." Cate stopped on the threshold, and Clay caught a faint whiff of some sweet, subtle scent wafting from her hair that kicked his pulse up a notch. "Where's your brother?"

Josh peeked around Emily's shoulder and smiled.

"How many pancakes did you eat?" Cate asked him.

He pondered, struggling through the math. "Four."

"No wonder you're such a big boy!"

He gave her a pleased grin, then he and Emily moved away from the door to allow her to enter.

Clay followed at a safe distance, shutting the door as he gave the room a swift survey, trying to see it through Cate's eyes. He spent so little time in the succession of apartments he'd occupied that he always opted for a small, furnished place—living room, efficiency kitchen, bedroom and bath. This was no exception.

Until today, Clay had thought the place was fine, if a bit cramped. But suddenly he recognized all its shortcomings. Besides being small, it was too sterile. There was nothing personal in the place to distinguish it from any unoccupied apartment in the complex. Nothing to suggest it was a home. Nothing warm and inviting. In other words, not the best environment for the children. Cate's expression, however, gave no hint of her reaction.

"Would you like some coffee?" he offered.

"No, thanks. But a glass of water would be great."

"Make yourself comfortable." He gestured toward the living room.

"I'd like to spend a few minutes with the children first, if you don't mind. I brought an activity for them. May I borrow your kitchen table?"

"Sure. Help yourself."

Cate followed him toward the kitchen, and as he got ice and water, she sat at the small table. The kids watched with interest as she withdrew a small tape recorder, a pad of paper and a box of crayons from her large shoulder tote.

"What's all that for?" Emily asked.

"I thought you might like to draw some pictures while I talk to your uncle." She tore off some sheets of paper and spread the crayons on the table. "The lady on the tape will tell you a story about a farmer and ask you to draw some of the things she talks about. After the tape ends, you can show me all your pictures."

"Emily draws good," Josh told Cate. "She drawed me a bird once."

"Today you'll both have a chance to draw lots of different animals. And a tractor and a barn and a big stalk of corn. And the sun and rain that make it grow."

After settling the children at the table, Cate started the tape player and listened to the beginning with them to ensure they understood the instructions.

From a few feet away, Clay watched, one hip propped against the counter. She had a way with kids, no question about it. They seemed to like and trust her. And she certainly knew how to keep them entertained. If they could work out a child care arrangement, he would be forever in Reverend Richards's debt.

And not just for the kids' sake, he realized. Though he knew little about the woman standing a few feet away, he felt comfortable in her presence. Reassured, somehow, that things would work out. He found her as appealing as his niece and nephew did—on a lot of levels, he acknowledged, watching her soft blond hair brush the gentle sweep of her cheek as she leaned close to help Josh select a crayon.

When Cate turned toward him, her slight blush told him she was aware he'd been staring. Not good, he berated himself. He needed her child care services, and making her nervous was *not* going to work in his favor.

Clearing his throat, he pushed away from the counter and inclined his head toward the living room.

He followed her into the adjacent room, noting as he took a chair at right angles to the couch that the volume of the tape was loud enough to mask their conversation. Add in the giggles of the children—a heartwarming sound he hadn't heard before—and it was clear they would be able to talk in privacy.

He was impressed.

"Good idea." He gestured toward the kitchen, keeping his voice low.

"Based on what you said this morning at church, I had a feeling there might be some things we needed to discuss that you didn't want them to hear. And it's not wise to send such young children outside to play alone. Especially in an apartment setting." She leaned forward slightly. "You mentioned this morning that you'd tried a local day care center, but it hadn't worked out?"

"It lasted all of two days. Josh had an…accident…both days during his nap, and they weren't willing to deal with a bedwetting four-year-old."

She frowned. "Does this happen often?"

"No. Emily says when he's upset he tends to have accidents at night. It's happened a couple of times."

"Losing their mother is more than enough to upset young children. Not to mention moving to a new place." Compassion softened Cate's features.

"To be honest, they've had far more trauma than that." Drawing a ragged breath, Clay gave her a brief overview of their life—and of his sister's death. As he spoke, the sympathy in Cate's eyes changed to shock, then horror.

"An environment like that can be so destructive to a child." She sent a concerned glance toward Emily and Josh. "It can take years to undo the damage."

"And I'm not the best person for the job. I'm on the move a lot, and I work long hours. Neither of which is conducive to family life."

"There's no one else who can take the children?"

"My father says they can live with him after he recovers from a bout of pneumonia. But my sister wouldn't have wanted that."

"May I ask why?"

Leaning forward, Clay rested his forearms on his thighs and clasped his hands between his knees. "My father isn't the warmest or kindest person in the world." He chose his words with care as he stared at the floor. "These kids would wither in his house. They need fun and laughter and love, and they won't get it there."

"Are you going to keep them?"

"I don't know." He raked his fingers through his hair, the familiar panic twisting his stomach into a knot. "I left home at seventeen, spent a dozen years in the Army, and I now have a job that takes me all over the country. I've been on my own for close to eighteen years, and I like it that way. I've never wanted a responsibility like this. As long as the kids are with me, though, I want to do my best to restore some semblance of childhood to their lives. But I can't do it alone. That's why I need your help."

Cate's gaze locked with his for a moment. Then she slung her tote bag over her shoulder and rose. "I need to give this a little thought, and pray about it. Can I call you later tonight?"

He stood, too, doing his best to rein in his escalating panic. Although he'd been concerned at first about Cate's disability, after talking with her and watching how she'd connected with Emily and Josh, he knew she would be perfect for them. But he understood her caution. She wouldn't be walking into the easiest situation. Yet they needed her, as surely as parched plants need water to survive.

"Look, is there anything I can say to convince you? I can give you the name of my sister's minister in Nebraska, or the police department, if you want to check out my story."

"I know how hard this must be for you." Her features gentled. "Give me a few hours. I'll have an answer for you tonight." She grasped her cane and stood. "I'd like to say goodbye to the children."

"Could I...would you mind giving me your phone number?" Clay didn't even try to hide his desperation.

"Of course." She recited her number as he jotted it down. "But I *will* call tonight."

He watched as she moved over to the table and gave each child's drawings her full attention, offering words of praise and encouragement. Their faces were more animated than Clay had ever seen them.

If he was the praying type, he'd get down on his knees the minute she left and ask God to make her decide in his favor. As it was, he simply sent a silent entreaty, a single eloquent word, to whoever in the cosmos might happen to be listening.

Please!

"Now tell us about that nice-looking man with the two adorable children I saw you talking to at church this morning." Cate's mother passed the basket of fresh-baked rolls to her daughter.

Cate had wondered how long it would take for someone in her family to grill her about that conversation. That was the one bad thing about being part of a close-knit clan. Everybody assumed they had a right to know everything about your life. On the plus side, however, her family had often proven to be a good sounding board.

"A man by the name of Clay Adams." She quickly filled them in on the situation.

"Poor man," her mother murmured.

"It might be better to go for a more permanent position," Mark offered as he helped himself to a second serving of roast chicken.

Her older brother had always been the most security-conscious sibling, and Cate wasn't surprised by his response. In light of his legal training, she also expected him to give her the third degree about Clay—unless Rob beat him to it.

"Sounds like this man could really use your help, though," her grandfather chimed in.

"The timing is perfect, too, since you're free now, anyway," her father added.

"It's odd how it worked out." Cate's face grew pensive. "I mean, he could have gone to any church, but he picked ours. And if he hadn't spoken to Pastor Bob, I would never have gotten involved. It's funny how a chance meeting can have such an impact."

"I'm not convinced it was chance," her mother declared. "I think it's all part of God's plan."

"Does this guy's story seem on the up-and-up to you?" Rob interjected.

"Spoken like a true police officer," Cate teased her younger brother.

"Hey, you can't be too careful these days."

"True. But he offered to put me in touch with the police department in his sister's hometown and her pastor."

"That's a good sign," Rob conceded. "If you ask me, I think you ought to help the guy out. He's new in town, has no family around and is trying to juggle what sounds like a demanding job with the needs of two kids. Speaking from the perspective of a single male, I imagine he's in way over his head and sinking fast."

"I think that's a fair assessment." Cate propped her chin in her hand and toyed with her mashed potatoes. "And the children are wonderful. But they need a lot of love and attention."

"Do you think it might be too much for you?" Her mother gave her a worried look.

"A challenge, maybe. But not too much."

"You'd be perfect for them," Michelle declared. "And I could help in a pinch, if things get crazy. It would be good practice." She patted her swelling tummy.

At her sister-in-law's comment, Cate smiled. "I think you're going to have other things on your mind for the next few months. But I appreciate the offer." She surveyed the table. "It sounds like the family consensus is that I should take the job."

"It would be the Christian thing to do," her mother said.

"What do *you* think, Cate?" her grandfather asked.

She sent him a grateful smile. Her opinionated family could be rather overwhelming, but Pop always managed to inject a subtle reminder that her decisions were, in the end, hers. They'd always been close, and the spry older man had been her staunchest ally when she'd decided to buy a condo despite the protests of her parents and her overly protective brothers.

"I'm going to pray on it a bit, but I think I'm going to do it. I sense a real need here. Besides, like Mom said, it would be the Christian thing to do."

"Whatever you decide will be the right thing." The conviction in Pop's tone ended the discussion. "Now where's that homemade apple pie?"

As the conversation shifted, Cate looked around at her family, the support system that had gotten her through the tough times. She'd always known she could count on them to lend a helping hand. That was a great blessing. One Clay Adams didn't have.

Perhaps, as her mother had suggested, their "chance" meeting today hadn't been chance at all, but part of God's plan. If it was, her decision seemed clear. But it couldn't hurt to ask for guidance.

Lord, if You don't think I'm the best person for this job, please let me know. And if You do want me to take it, I ask for strength and wisdom as I deal with these traumatized children. Because helping them heal, giving them a sense of security, bringing joy and laughter back into their lives, will be the biggest challenge of my career. And I don't want to fail.

Chapter Three

"We're going to the park tomorrow to fly a kite," Emily told Clay as she handed him a dinner plate to add to the load in the dishwasher.

He rinsed the plate. "We don't have a kite."

"Yes, we do. Cate stopped at the store today and got one."

Clay frowned. He'd told Cate to keep track of expenses, but ten days into the job she'd only requested reimbursement for groceries. Although he hadn't asked her to take on shopping and cooking chores, he was grateful she had. His kitchen was now stocked with fresh vegetables, healthy frozen entrees and home-cooked casseroles.

But if she was buying other things—like kites—for the children, he needed to pay her back for those, too. He made a mental note to discuss it with her.

Clay picked up the plate of fresh-baked chocolate chip cookies from the table…another perk of Cate's employment.

"Emily and me helped make those," Josh offered.

"You did a great job, buddy." Clay smiled and took another cookie. "They're the best chocolate chip cookies I've ever had. Did you see how many I ate?"

"Bunches," Josh said.

The corners of Clay's mouth hitched up. "Too true. Emily, are you finished with your milk?" He reached for her glass.

"No!" Her hand shot out, knocking the glass over and sending a stream of white liquid surging across the kitchen table. Anxiety tightened her features, but at least she didn't cringe as Josh had when he'd spilled his milk the day after they'd arrived. Clay hoped that meant he was making progress toward his goal of convincing the children that not all men reacted with anger to mistakes, like their father had. But it was slow going.

"I'm sorry." Emily's words came out hesitant and soft.

Clay sopped up the spilled milk with a dish towel, dropped into a chair to put himself at her level—a technique he'd picked up from Cate—and held out his hand. He'd discovered that quick movements caused the children to recoil in fear and had learned to let them make the connection.

"It's okay, Emily. It was a mistake. Easy to fix. We have plenty of milk."

After considering his outstretched hand, she inched hers across the table. As she made tentative contact, he enfolded her small fingers in his and gave them a gentle, reassuring squeeze.

"Tell me about this kite flying." He refilled her glass and set it in front of her before sitting back at the table with his cup of coffee.

"We saw some kids flying kites in the park today, and we asked Cate if we could do that, too. She said she was a little…" Emily squinted in concentration, trying to remember the word.

"Russy," Josh supplied.

"What does that mean?" Emily sent Clay a quizzical look.

"I think she probably said 'rusty.'" Clay tried to stifle his smile. "It means out of practice."

"Oh. Anyway, she said she was a little rusty, but we'd give it a try. We stopped at the store and got a kite on the way home."

"I'll show it to you." Josh scampered into the bedroom, returning a minute later with an inexpensive kite kit. "We have to put it together."

"Do you want to do that now?"

"Can we?" Josh asked eagerly.

"Sure."

Fifteen minutes later, Clay held the bright red kite aloft for the children to admire.

"Wow!" Josh regarded it in awe. "Cate says we have to run like the wind to make it fly."

Even though Cate had put her cane aside and was moving much better than the day they'd met, her limp was still apparent. And the children's legs were too short to allow them to run fast enough to get the kite airborne. How was she planning to get this aloft? Clay wondered.

"When are you going to fly it?" he asked.

"Cate says before lunch." Josh touched the kite in wonder.

"I'm finished with my milk now." Emily handed Clay her empty glass.

He added it to the dishwasher. "Okay. Bath time."

The bedtime ritual was still too unfamiliar to him to be done by rote, but once the children were settled, Clay's thoughts returned to Cate rather than the unfinished work he'd brought home. He hadn't known her very long. And he didn't know her well. Their exchanges had been confined to a few words in the morning and evening, and a quick hello at church on Sunday. But he admired her. Not only for her kindness and consideration with the children, but for her strength and endurance. Despite the harsh, unfair blow life had dealt her, she'd managed to make her peace with it and move on. And she didn't let it stop her from living as normal a life as possible.

That's why he was worried. If she wanted to fly a kite, Clay was certain she'd find a way to do it.

But he didn't want her to get hurt in the process.

Cate knotted the last piece of colorful cotton cloth onto the kite's tail and held it out for the children to inspect. "What do you think?"

"It's pretty." Emily touched it with reverence. "Do you think it will fly?"

"There's only one way to find out." She handed it to Pop. "Are you ready to do the honors for this inaugural flight?"

"I haven't flown a kite in years, but I don't think I've lost the touch. Emily, why don't you hold the kite. Josh, you take the tail."

Caution suppressing their enthusiasm, they did as he instructed in silence. Cate was glad she'd asked Pop to help today. Clay had assured her the children's father hadn't hurt them, and her own gentle probing with them had led her to the same conclusion. But it was clear they'd been afraid of him. And they'd transferred that fear to all men.

They were better now with Clay. She could see their tension slowly easing when they were around him. Enough that she'd decided it was time to expand their horizons. And Pop was the perfect next step.

"Okay, I think we're all set," he declared.

He led the way to the open field, positioning Emily with her hands aloft, lifting the kite into the wind, while Josh took up the rear, holding the tail above the ground. Unwinding string as he walked, he moved a few feet away.

"Okay. On the count of three, let the kite go, Emily. You too, Josh. One, two…" Pop started jogging, "three!"

As Cate watched from a bench, Emily and Josh released the kite and tail, and it soared for a brief glorious moment.

Then it crashed to the ground.

Pop stopped and rewound the string as he worked his way back to the kite. "Don't worry," he assured the disappointed children. "They don't always fly the first time. Let's give it another try."

Their second attempt produced the same results. Three tries later, after adding some additional tail and moving to a different spot, they were no closer to getting it aloft. But their less-than-successful efforts had broken down the barriers between the children and Pop. The three of them were now chatting like old friends.

Cate watched as Pop examined the kite. He was in great shape for his age, but she didn't want him to overexert himself.

"Maybe it's not a good kite." Josh examined it in disgust.

"Kite's fine," Pop declared, huffing as he checked it over. "Must be the pilot."

Stepping in, Cate reached for the kite. "Go rest for a minute while I take a look at it."

He handed over the kite, shook his head and planted his fists on his hips. "Can't figure it out. Wind's good. Kite's strong. Should have flown."

"Go sit." Cate grinned and gave him a firm push. "Let the expert take over."

The twinkle in his eye mitigated his indignant tone. "Expert, huh? I'll have you know I was a champion kite flyer in my younger days."

"Okay, okay, you can try again in a minute. In the meantime, go sit."

"I'll be back," he told the children. "We'll get this baby up yet."

As he headed for a nearby bench Emily leaned toward Cate and spoke in a whisper. "I don't think it's going to fly."

Cate considered the kite. In general, she didn't attempt any activity that required her to run, but her leg felt strong today. She wouldn't have to go far. A few steps, at the most. She was sure she could get the kite to soar with very little effort. The temptation to give it a try herself was too strong to resist.

Ignoring the warning that began to flash in her mind, she turned to the children. "Emily, you hold the kite again. Josh, you take the tail. Let's show Pop who the real champion kite flyers are."

The children's eyes lit up. Cate saw Pop rise from the bench, but she ignored him. "Okay. One, two," she began to run, "three!"

Emily and Josh released the kite, and Cate ran as she hadn't run in years. Not with her old grace or speed. But she was running. And it felt great!

Until she stepped onto an uneven spot in the ground and pitched forward.

As Cate fell, she released the kite string and tried to brace herself for the impact. But the new spring grass didn't offer much cushion from the hard ground. When her hands connected with the earth, a shaft of pain shot up her left arm.

And she knew she'd made a big mistake.

Clay consulted his watch, took off his hard hat, and stuck his head in the door of the construction trailer. "I'm taking an early lunch today, Becky. I should be back in an hour."

The office manager grinned. "Hot date?"

"Yeah. With a kite."

"Huh?" She sent him a puzzled look.

"The kids got a new kite yesterday. They were going to fly it before lunch. I thought I'd run over to the park and surprise them."

"They must be getting under your skin." She gave him a smirk.

He quirked a brow and ignored her comment. "See you later."

But she was right, he acknowledged as he drove to the park. The kids were getting under his skin. He enjoyed their innocent questions, took pleasure in eliciting their smiles. And it gave him a good feeling to watch their haunted look fade day by day— thanks in large part to Cate's gentle ministrations.

He hadn't had a chance this morning to talk to her about reimbursement for the kite, or quiz her about how she planned to get it aloft. He'd had an emergency page from the job site as she'd arrived and had flown out the door the instant she'd stepped inside. The crisis had kept him busy all morning. But he'd blocked out time to take an early lunch and go fly a kite with them instead of letting Cate put herself at risk.

As he pulled into the park, he slowed his speed, scanning the grounds. He didn't see Cate, but the movement of an older man rising from a bench caught his attention. His tense posture put Clay on alert, and he followed the man's line of sight—to Cate and the children.

She was holding the kite, and as he pulled into a parking space he saw the children grasp it. They backed up, and a tingle of apprehension raced down his spine. He set the brake and climbed out of his truck, striding toward the small group as Cate started to run.

Considering her lameness, he was surprised at how fast she could move. His step slowed as his appreciative gaze followed her willowy, jeans-clad form across the spring grass. And the radiant joy on her face took his breath away.

But in the next moment, what little breath remained in his lungs came out in a whoosh as she stumbled and fell. Headlong and hard. His heart stopped for an instant, and then his adrenaline surged, propelling him forward.

Seconds later he was beside her, well ahead of the children

or the older man he'd noticed earlier. She had rolled to her side and lay curled into a ball, cradling her hand.

Dropping down on one knee, he touched her shoulder. "Cate?" Her name came out in a hoarse whisper.

She blinked up at him in confusion. "Clay? What are you doing here?"

"I was going to help you fly the kite. I see I'm too late." She struggled to sit up, but he restrained her. "I'm not sure you should move until we know if you're hurt."

"I'm okay." She shrugged off his hand as she sat. "I just twisted my wrist. I'll be fine." She looked over his shoulder and managed a shaky smile. "We almost got it up, didn't we?"

He turned. Emily had grown pale, and Josh was huddled beside her. The older man stood behind them, a comforting hand resting on each of their shoulders.

"It-it flied real good for a minute." Josh's words were quavery.

"Did you hurt your leg again?" Emily sounded close to tears.

"No. It's okay."

She attempted to stand, and again Clay restrained her. "Are you sure you're okay?" He kept his volume low. Partly because he didn't want to further distress the children. And partly because he didn't trust his voice.

Angling her head toward him, she opened her mouth to speak…but nothing came out.

Staring into her gorgeous eyes mere inches away, Clay misplaced his voice, too. Fringed by long, sweeping lashes, their green depths were flecked with gold, he realized. And that wasn't all he noticed. Beneath his fingers, her shoulders felt delicate and soft. A capricious breeze ruffled her hair, and without stopping to think, he brushed it back from her cheek, letting the silky strands drift through his fingers as his mouth went dry.

The older man cleared his throat, breaking the spell. "You okay, honey?"

With an obvious effort, Cate directed her attention behind Clay again, a slow flush creeping across her cheeks. "Yes. I'm fine." Her breathless reassurance, however, wasn't at all credible. "Pop, this is Clay Adams. Clay, my grandfather." As she did the introductions, she glanced at Clay briefly.

Forcing himself to break contact, Clay rose and held out his hand. "Nice to meet you, sir."

"Likewise." Pop's grip was firm, his eyes shrewd and discerning.

As Cate began to stand, Clay turned to support her. She leaned into him, cradling her wrist, a grimace of pain pulling her features taut.

"We need to have that checked out."

"No. I have some ace bandages at home that will take care of it." She tipped her chin up to look at him, her eyes anxious. "Sorry about this. I know my limits, and I try not to take foolish chances, but once in a while I forget. In most cases, I live to regret it. Like today. It doesn't mean I can't take good care of the children."

"I know that." At the conviction in his voice, the tension in her face eased. Good. He didn't want her worrying about his confidence in her.

Next, he addressed the children, who were still too subdued and quiet. "Why don't we all go out to lunch?"

"Could we get hamburgers?" Emily asked, brightening.

"And French fries?" Josh added.

"Sure." He turned to Cate's grandfather. "You're welcome to join us, too, sir."

The older man, who had been watching the exchange with interest, shook his head. "Make it Pop. Everyone else does. And

I'll take a rain check on the burger. The garden club meeting starts in an hour and I have to swing by the house and pick up a few things." He bent down to the children, hands on knees. "We're not going to give up on this kite. On the next windy day, we have a date."

Emily and Josh sent Cate an uncertain, but hopeful, glance.

"That sounds good," she agreed with a smile. "And next trip, I'll stay on the sidelines. I promise." She aimed her final remark at Clay.

"Maybe I'll come, too," he said.

"Our daddy never did anything like that with us." There was a hint of melancholy in Emily's tone.

Clay dropped down to balance beside them on the balls of his feet. "That's too bad. He missed a lot of fun." Squeezing her hand and ruffling Josh's hair, he rose. "Okay, let's see about that lunch."

As they walked toward the parking area, Clay realized Cate's limp was more pronounced than usual. But he knew she was making a valiant effort to hide it for the sake of the children, trying to reassure them everything was okay.

He understood her motivation. He felt the same need to protect the kids. While it was a new feeling for him, he found it surprisingly appealing.

Even more surprising, however, was the protective feeling he felt about Cate. That, too, was appealing. But scary. Very scary.

Suddenly she stumbled, lurching against him, and his arm shot out to steady her. She murmured a soft thank-you and tried to move away, but he slipped his arm around her shoulders again.

"Relax and lean on me," he said close to her ear. "There's no sense putting any extra strain on your leg."

For an instant, she stiffened. But in the end she complied— leading Clay to assume she was hurting more than she'd let on.

Cate didn't strike him as the kind of woman who leaned on people very often.

There was no opportunity to analyze her response, however, because all at once Clay felt small fingers slipping into his other hand. Josh looked up at him, one finger in his mouth as he trotted beside his uncle, ready to jerk his hand free if his overture met with a negative reaction.

A wave of tenderness washed over Clay, and he tried to blink away the hot tears welling in his eyes. Mere weeks ago this little boy had been too traumatized to speak, isolating himself from everyone but Emily. While much work remained to be done, Clay knew Josh's reaching out, testing the waters, was a sign of great progress. That the healing had started. And with the help of the woman beside him, it would continue.

Once in the parking lot, Pop lifted a hand in farewell. "We'll get that kite up yet," he promised the children.

As Pop slid into his car, Clay looked at Cate. And tried not to drown in those green pools she called eyes. "Why don't we take my truck to lunch?"

Cate moistened her lips with the tip of her tongue, drawing his attention to them. Once more, his mouth went dry.

"Okay." Her reply came out in a throaty voice he'd never heard before.

They set off toward his truck, and when Josh tugged free to climb up, Clay felt bereft without the boy's small hand tucked in his. It was also time to remove his arm from Cate's shoulder, Clay knew.

But for a man who valued his independence and had avoided commitments for his entire adult life, the oddest thing happened.

He didn't want to let her go.

* * *

It was time for more aspirin.

With a slight moan, Cate swung her legs to the floor and peered at her bedside clock. Three in the morning. She had to be back at Clay's in four and a half hours, and so far she'd logged no more than two hours of sleep.

Shuffling toward the bathroom, cane in hand and aching all over after her kite-flying caper yesterday, she tried to attribute her sleeplessness to her physical discomfort.

But she knew that was only part of it.

The bulk of the blame rested on Clay.

As she rummaged bleary-eyed through the drawers in the bathroom vanity, she tried to analyze why a man she hadn't even known existed three weeks ago could wreak havoc on her sleep, filling her nights with restless dreams that left her feeling unsettled come morning.

Early on, she'd attributed her reaction to chemistry. But that didn't quite ring true anymore. Not that the chemistry wasn't there, though. Despite the fact that Clay wasn't the type who usually attracted her, she couldn't dismiss that stomach flutter thing. It happened every time he was around. Nor could she ignore the way her nerve endings tingled whenever he came within three feet of her.

But it was more than chemistry.

For whatever reason, the rootless, commitment-averse engineer who had zero tolerance for religion and came from a dysfunctional family had touched her heart.

She supposed his innate kindness, demonstrated in simple gestures, played a role in her reaction. Like the rubber toys she'd found propped on the edge of his bathtub. And the Disney night-light he'd installed in the room—his room—where the children slept. And the way he listened to their prayers at night, despite his own feelings about religion. Emily had told her about that.

His unselfishness touched her, too. He slept on an uncomfortable couch. He brought unfinished work home instead of staying late at the office, toiling on it long after the children went to bed. He never failed to take them to church.

There was a lot to like about Clay.

And if things were different…

Shaking the aspirin into her palm with more force than necessary, Cate ruthlessly cut off that line of thought. Things weren't different. There was no way anything could ever develop between them, no matter the chemistry. For two very good reasons, she reminded herself, as she downed the aspirin in one gulp and headed back to bed.

First, a man like Clay could have his pick of women. He didn't need to settle for one who was disabled.

Second, even if by some remote chance he was attracted to her, he'd made it clear he had no interest in a serious, committed relationship.

And as far as she was concerned, that was the only kind worth having.

End of story.

Chapter Four

Cate heard Emily crying inside the apartment before she ever reached the landing, a close-to-hysterical wailing that knotted her stomach and set her adrenaline pumping.

Taking the last two steps as quickly as she could given her aches and pains from yesterday's fall, Cate crossed the landing, inserted her key in the lock and stepped inside.

Chaos greeted her.

The children were still in their pajamas. Emily was in Clay's arms, quivering—and clinging to his neck with such fierceness he could hardly move his head. Josh was huddled into a ball in the corner of the sofa, legs pulled up, tears flowing down his pale, frightened face as he watched the tableau a few steps away.

Clay didn't look much better. He wore only a white T-shirt and jeans, his hair was uncombed and a full day's growth of beard darkened his jaw. He was bouncing Emily gently in his arms, murmuring soothing words, but the face he turned toward her when she crossed the threshold was bewildered —and bordering on frantic.

"I'm so glad you're here!" Relief hoarsened his voice.

"What happened?" Cate dropped her sweater on a chair and joined the troubled trio.

"I have no idea. We were eating breakfast, I gave Emily a piece of toast and she freaked." He had to raise his voice to be heard above the child's weeping.

"How long has this been going on?"

"I don't know. Ten minutes, maybe. I can't calm her down."

Moving around Clay, Cate lifted a hand to stroke Emily's tangled hair. One of the little girl's cheeks was pressed against her uncle's neck, and she'd bunched the cotton fabric of his T-shirt into her clenched fists. Her legs were locked around his torso, her cheeks were splotchy, and terror and anguish had glazed her eyes.

"Emily, honey, it's okay. Can you tell me what's wrong? Does your tummy hurt?"

No response. Cate wasn't even sure her presence had registered in the child's consciousness. She was lost in some fear-filled world of her own.

"Clay, can you sit on the couch?"

He did so in silence, perching on the edge of the seat cushion.

Easing down beside Josh, Cate took the little boy's cold hand. He needed attention, too, but her first priority had to be calming Emily. And perhaps Josh could give them a clue to the source of her distress.

"Josh, would you like me to hold you?"

The little boy responded by climbing into her lap. Cuddling his little body close, Cate stroked his fine blond hair.

"Why is Emily c-crying?" Josh hiccupped the word, giving Cate a distraught look.

"I don't know, honey. I think something scared her."

"Maybe the t-toast." He reached out a pudgy finger to touch Emily's cheek, his eyelashes spiky with moisture. "Don't cry, Em."

Clay shifted, homing in on the boy's comment. "What about the toast, Josh?"

"She burnt it."

From his baffled expression, it was obvious Clay had no idea why this was relevant, Cate deduced.

"Is that a bad thing, Josh?" Cate kept her tone gentle as she wrapped the little boy in a soothing hug.

"Yes. Our toaster at home d-didn't work too good. Mommy got hurt a lot, and when she had to stay in bed Emily made us toast f-for breakfast. But it always burnt and the kitchen got stinky. Daddy d-didn't like that."

Although Emily's wails had quieted to a whimper, her grip on Clay's neck hadn't loosened.

Cate began to get a glimmer of the reason for today's meltdown. "What would happen then?" She stroked the back of Emily's hand in a reassuring, rhythmic motion as she asked Josh the question. A shudder ran through the little girl, and Clay patted her back, rubbing his cheek against the top of her head.

His lip quivering, Josh nestled closer to Cate. "He would open all the windows, even if it was really cold. And he'd m-make Emily stand on the b-back porch without her coat until the kitchen smelled better. There was a big, mean, scary d-dog that came to our alley s-sometimes, but no matter how h-hard Emily pounded on the d-door, Daddy wouldn't let her back in. One time the d-dog tore her shirt."

Clay stiffened. Emily emitted a soft whimper, and Cate laid a warning hand on his arm.

"Well, there are no bad dogs around here, so we can all relax." She emphasized the last word, and Clay got the message.

He managed to slacken his muscles, and Emily let out a slow, ragged breath.

"Why did our daddy do that?" Confused, Josh stuck his thumb in his mouth and tipped his head back to study her.

Wishing there was an easy answer, Cate worded her response with care. "Some people aren't very nice and they do bad things for no reason. Daddies are supposed to love their families and take care of them, not be mean. Your daddy made some bad mistakes. But you're with your Uncle Clay now, and he loves you very much. I do, too. So now that you're here, you don't have to worry about people being mean to you. We would never let that happen."

Emily's grip on Clay's neck eased.

"Did they eat breakfast?" Cate asked Clay in a quiet, conversational tone.

He shook his head.

"Do you have half an hour to spare?"

"Whatever it takes."

"I have an idea," Cate told the children. "Why don't we make chocolate chip pancakes for breakfast?"

"I never heard of those." Emily shifted her position to better see Cate without relinquishing her hold on Clay.

"No one has. They're my secret recipe. But I can't make them by myself. It takes four people. One to mix, one to add in the chocolate chips, one to flip, and one to pour the chocolate syrup on top."

"Chocolate syrup, too? Wow!" Josh's eyes lit up. "I'll help!"

"So will I," Clay seconded.

"Emily? Are you in?" Cate smiled at her.

The little girl nodded.

"Good. Let's get started, then."

Half an hour later, as the children were lingering over the last bites of their unusual breakfast, Clay glanced toward the clock on the wall and raised an eyebrow at Cate. He'd disappeared once during breakfast to shave, put on his shirt and comb his hair, and she knew he was running way behind schedule.

Rising unhurriedly, she took her plate to the sink. "I saw a mama duck with some baby ducks the other day as I drove past the park, and I bet they're still there. While Uncle Clay's at work today, how would you like to go feed them?"

"Yes!" Josh said. "Can we go now?"

"As soon as you get dressed."

He scrambled off his chair. "I can be ready in two minutes."

Smiling, Cate grabbed his pajama top as he dashed by. "Whoa. Say goodbye to your uncle first."

Josh planted a sloppy kiss on Clay's cheek. "Bye. Come on, Emily!" He dashed down the hall.

Sliding off her chair, Emily looked less enthusiastic.

"How about a hug?" Clay held out his arms, and she moved toward him. "I'll be back in time for supper, okay?"

"Can't you stay home today?"

He shot Cate a quick glance. "I won't be far away. I can come home if you need me, and Cate will be here all day, like always. I'll tell you what. Why don't you call me from the park and tell me about the ducks? Would you do that?"

"Okay, I guess." Backing out of the circle of his arms, she traipsed down the hall.

As Clay headed for the front door, Cate followed. They stepped onto the landing, and she left the door slightly ajar so she could listen for the children.

Running his fingers through the hair he'd just combed, Clay let out a frustrated breath. "I wish I could stay home today."

"They'll be okay. Don't worry."

As he regarded her, his eyes softened. "They wouldn't be if

it wasn't for you. I was way over my head when you walked in the door."

His praise warmed her heart. More than it should. "You would have been fine."

"I don't think so. You did all the right things. Asked the right questions. When I think what that monster did to those two..." His face hardened.

"It's hard to believe a man could treat his own children that way." Cate's throat tightened, and she blinked away the sudden moisture that blurred her vision.

"My dad was bad. But nothing like Martin." Clay pulled his keys out of his pocket. "You'll call me from the park?"

"Absolutely."

"Okay." He gave her the semblance of a smile. "The chocolate chip pancakes were inspired, by the way. A very clever way to distract the kids."

"I'm glad it worked. I was making it up as I went along."

He shook his head. "That's what I mean. I would never have thought of something like that." Warmth flooded his deep brown eyes, and Cate's pulse took a leap. "I've never been very good about saying thank-you, or expressing my feelings, but I want you to know how much I appreciate everything you've done for us."

His husky, intimate tone blindsided her, and she had to force her uncooperative lungs to kick in. Standing inches away, the morning sun bronzing his skin, Clay oozed a potent masculinity that made her lightheaded. Unless she was way off base, he felt the powerful chemistry between them, too. Because what she saw in his eyes represented a far deeper emotion than the appreciation he'd verbalized.

As if to confirm her conclusion, he lifted a hand toward her. She held her breath, every nerve in her body quivering. She knew she should step back. But she couldn't move. With every fiber of her being, she wanted to feel the touch of his strong, work-toughened fingers against her cheek. Without conscious decision, she swayed toward him, inviting him to…

"Cate!" The door was pulled open, and she jerked back as Josh scurried out. "I'm ready to go feed the ducks."

Reeling from the rush of emotion, Cate looked toward the little boy. He was dressed—sort of—in jeans, an unbuttoned shirt and mismatched shoes without socks. Any other time, she'd have gotten a chuckle out of his slapdash attire. At the moment, though, it was all she could do to get her tongue to work.

"I'll be right in, Josh. Why don't you go put some socks on?"

He checked out his feet. "Oh. I guess I forgot."

Whirling around, he dashed back inside.

When Cate managed to summon up enough courage to face Clay again, she discovered he'd moved to the railing and shoved his palms flat in the back pockets of his jeans.

He swallowed, and she watched his Adam's apple bob. "I better go."

All she could manage was a nod.

He left in silence.

Thirty seconds later, she heard his car door slam. The engine started. She stepped back into the shadows and caught sight of his car as he backed out. The receding sound of the engine told her he'd gone.

Leaving disappointment in his wake.

But it was better this way, she told herself. Business and pleasure didn't mix. Had Clay touched her, things between them would have changed. That wouldn't have been good for any of them—Clay, her or the children.

Yet hard as she tried to convince herself that Josh's interruption had been a good thing, her heart wasn't buying the argument.

* * *

"Clay!"

As his name rang out across the quiet morning air two days later, Clay stopped. Cate and her grandfather were coming down the church steps, and she waved.

He returned the gesture, but stayed where he was. Since Emily's meltdown, he'd been off balance around Cate. He still couldn't believe how close he'd come to kissing her that day on the landing. With the gilded light of morning turning her hair into a shimmering halo and her deep green eyes misting with compassion, he'd been overwhelmed by a rush of unfamiliar, tender emotions.

And he'd almost made a big mistake.

Cate wasn't the kind of woman a man kissed lightly. Clay knew that. With her gentle goodness and caring nature, she'd expect such an intimate gesture to signify more than a momentary attraction. And that's all it had been, he told himself. Prompted by gratitude for her role in dealing with the morning crisis.

But that didn't help him keep said attraction in line as he watched her walk toward him, dressed in a simple sheath dress and matching jacket that flattered her figure and highlighted the slender curves of her five-foot-six frame.

"Do you have a minute?" Cate greeted him with a smile.

She seemed to have put the Friday morning incident behind her, he noted, struggling to do the same. "Sure." The word came out ragged, and he cleared his throat.

"Have you two seen the ducks yet?" Pop directed his question to the children.

"There are ducks at church? Like at the park?" Josh's eyes widened.

"Mmm hmm. In a little pond out back. How about we check it out?"

"Okay," Josh agreed promptly.

Emily hesitated and looked up at Clay. "Is it all right?"

"Yes. But don't be gone too long."

"We'll be back in a jiffy," Pop promised. The older man reached for their hands, and the children slipped their fingers into his without a qualm.

Clay shoved his hands into his pockets as he watched them. "Must run in the family."

"What?" Cate gave him a quizzical look.

"The ability to get along with children. They've only met your grandfather what…twice?…and already they trust him. It's taking me a lot longer."

"Pop's had a lot of practice with children. I have, too. But you're doing great. And the children are making good progress."

He gave a rueful shake of his head. "Based on what happened Friday, they have a long way to go."

"I have an idea that might speed up their healing process."

"I'm all for that."

"It occurred to me that some exposure to happy family life might be good for them. My mom always has everyone over for Easter brunch, and we wondered if you and the children would like to join us next Sunday."

Considering how adamant Cate had been about her ground rules when she'd accepted the job, he was taken aback. "I thought you wanted to keep your weekends to yourself."

"In general, I do." A soft flush spread across her cheeks, and she tucked her hair behind her ear. "But Easter is a special day. Worthy of an exception. Besides, it would be good for the children."

He mulled over the invitation. Since he'd left home, Easter had never been more to him than another Sunday to sleep in. He'd go to church this year for the children's sake, but he hadn't planned to mark the day in any other way. Yet Cate's suggestion reminded him he should make an effort to celebrate the holiday. Kids were supposed to get baskets of candy and colored eggs, weren't they? And a special dinner? He could take care of the former. Cate was offering to provide the latter. And it would be good for the kids, as she'd noted.

Besides, the notion of spending a day in her company appealed to him on a personal level as well.

"That sounds very nice. Thank you. I'm sure the kids will enjoy it."

"Great." A smile curved her graceful lips. "I can give you details next week and…"

"Good morning, Cate."

An attractive blond man, accompanied by a dark-haired woman holding a baby, stopped beside them. Cate's smile disappeared, and some unidentifiable emotion flashed across her face, come and gone with such speed Clay wondered if he'd imagined it.

"Hello, Dan, Mary." As she introduced them to Clay, he caught the hint of sadness deep in her eyes.

The two men shook hands, and Clay inclined his head toward the woman, trying to get a handle on the odd vibes swirling around the small group.

"I wondered if I could ask you a favor, Cate," Dan said. "I have to go to St. Louis for a meeting Wednesday night, and I need someone to cover the youth group. I know you haven't done it since…" he cleared his throat "…for a while, but you know the ropes and I could use your help."

"I'd be happy to."

"Thanks. I owe you." The man flushed and ran a finger around the collar of his dress shirt.

Pop rejoined them, giving the couple a curt nod. "Dan, Mary."

At the out-of-character coolness in Pop's voice, Clay's antennae rose another notch.

As the couple said goodbye, Josh tugged on Clay's hand. "Pop says he'll take us fishing, if that's okay with you. Can we go?"

"I don't see why not." He transferred his attention from the young couple to Josh. "Maybe I'll come, too. If I'm invited."

"'Course you're invited," Pop said. "We'll take a picnic. Cate could join us, too."

"Would you, Cate?"

At Emily's question, Cate blinked and gave the little girl a blank look. "I'm sorry, honey. What did you say?"

"Pop said he'll take us fishing. And Uncle Clay is coming. It's going to be a picnic. Can you come, too?"

"Sure." Cate gave her a smile, but it seemed forced. "That sounds like fun. As soon as the weather warms up a little, we'll go out to the lake. And in the meantime, we have a surprise for you."

That was his cue to tell the children about Easter, Clay realized. He knelt on one knee beside them. "How would you guys like to have Easter dinner with Cate and her family?"

"Does Cate have a family?" Josh scrunched up his face, as he grappled with that concept.

"Of course. She has a grandpa—Pop—and a mommy and a daddy and…" He searched his memory, trying to recall what she'd told him about her family… "And two brothers and a sister-in-law." He glanced at her for confirmation, and she nodded.

"What's a sister-in-law?" Emily wanted to know.

"That's a lady who's married to one of Cate's brothers."

Josh scuffed the toe of his shoe, his eyes downcast, his tone subdued. "That's a lot of people. And we don't know them."

"You will after Easter."

After a moment, Josh tipped his head back and spoke to Cate. "Is your daddy nice?"

She dropped down to their level. Clay took her arm in a steadying grip and tried to ignore the appealing warmth of her skin radiating through the fabric of her thin jacket. "He's very nice, Josh. He likes little boys and girls. Just like Pop. Pop is my mommy's daddy."

Josh digested that, inspecting Pop. "You're a daddy, too?"

"That's right."

"Well…I guess it would be okay."

"What do you think?" Clay gave Emily a chance to cast her vote.

"Will you be there?"

"Yes."

"Okay."

It was okay because he would be with them.

As the significance of her statement sank in, Clay felt a new and unexpected joy spring to life within him. And when Cate smiled and touched his arm, acknowledging the moment as well, the joy in his heart spilled over.

He could get used to this happy feeling, Clay realized. And though he'd spent a lifetime avoiding personal attachments, with their confining obligations and responsibilities, as he gazed at Josh and Emily and Cate he didn't feel trapped at all.

He just felt good.

But scared.

Even more scared than the time he'd lost his balance on a structural steel beam and almost plunged six floors to the ground.

Since that near-accident, he always double-checked his safety harness before stepping into a danger zone.

Unfortunately, he didn't think there was any such protective equipment for the heart.

Chapter Five

"Would anyone like another piece of cake?"

Though her question was directed to the group gathered around the Shepard table, Cate's mother focused on the children. They'd each had two servings of Easter ham, devoured her au gratin potatoes and put a good dent in her green bean casserole. Clay had lost track of the number of homemade biscuits they'd eaten.

Both Emily and Josh sent Clay a hopeful look.

"I might take you up on your offer. But only if Josh and Emily do, too." Clay winked at Cate's mother and addressed the children. "Do you think you might be able to eat another piece?"

"I can," Josh declared with a vigorous nod.

"Me, too," Emily added.

"I think you have three takers on this side of the table. The dinner was wonderful, Mrs. Shepard."

"I'm glad you enjoyed it. And please call me Ellen."

While Cate's mother dished up multiple second servings of her home-baked split-lemon cake, Clay found his attention wandering to Cate. She was talking to her brother, teasing him about some childhood memory, and the animated sparkle in her eye reminded him, for a brief instant, of Anne in her carefree, light-hearted moments.

But those brief interludes had been rare. Most of the time she'd chaffed under the rigid, joyless regime of their youth, sharing his desperation to flee from their father's house. But she'd chosen a different escape route. Anne had wanted to create her own warm and loving family, perhaps to compensate for all she'd missed as a child. He, on the other hand, had wanted to stay as far away from family life as possible.

Clay had always been confident he'd chosen the better path. But this past month with Josh and Emily—and Cate—had shaken his conviction.

As if sensing his scrutiny, Cate looked toward him. The connection lasted no more than a fleeting instant, yet Clay had a feeling she saw far more than he'd intended to reveal.

"Another wonderful dinner, honey." Cate's father smiled at his wife as he rose and began clearing the table. Her brothers followed suit.

Noting Clay's surprise, Ellen explained. "In the Shepard clan, the women have always been the cooks and the men take care of clean-up duty. It's a good arrangement, don't you think?"

Yes, it was. But in his father's house, his mother had done all the cooking *and* all the clean-up. Likewise in Anne's home, from what she'd told him. He'd assumed all families operated that way.

"Seems logical to me. Let me help."

"Guests are excluded from that rule." She waved his offer aside as he started to rise. "Cate, why don't you show Clay and the children the pond your dad built? The fish are getting active again."

"You have a lake with fish in your yard?" Josh sought confirmation from Cate.

"Well, 'lake' is a pretty generous term. But it's a nice little pond. And it does have fish. Let me grab a sweater." Cate stood and headed for the hall.

"Come on into the family room while we wait," Ellen suggested.

As Clay followed Cate's mother to the back of the house, which was more casual and homey than the formal living room where they'd gathered earlier, he examined the photos lining the walls. They showed the Shepards celebrating birthdays, vacations, graduations—in other words, all the moments that wove the tapestry of a good family life. And there were pictures of each of the children, the kind most parents displayed. Such photos had been kept in a drawer in his father's house, however. Putting them out for others to see would have been a sin of pride, the old man had told them.

Clay's step slowed as he examined the photos of the three siblings. Mark was in sports attire, holding a soccer ball beside a trophy labeled "state champions." Rob wore a hockey uniform, his goalie mask tilted back to reveal his broad grin. No surprises there. Her brothers struck him as the athletic type.

But the last shot brought him to an abrupt halt.

It was Cate, dressed in a gossamer white tutu, her long legs encased in tights, one hand arced over her head, the other forming a half circle at waist level. She was balanced *en pointe* on one foot, her other leg extended toward the camera and bent gracefully at the knee, her slender, supple form the epitome of elegance, grace and poise. She wore her hair in traditional ballerina fashion, pulled back into a bun and surrounded by some sort of feathery headpiece. Her face was radiant and filled with joy, her beautiful bone structure enhanced by the classic hair style.

She was, in a word, stunning.

"She's lovely, isn't she?" Ellen said, as if reading his thoughts. "That's her dancing the leading role in *Swan Lake* at eighteen."

Meaning this must have been taken right before she was stricken with Guillain-Barre Syndrome, Clay concluded with a jolt.

Ellen spoke again, confirming his conclusion. "Two weeks after she danced this role, she got sick. Only a few days before she was supposed to leave for New York."

"She was going to New York?"

"I guess I'm not surprised she hasn't mentioned it." Ellen sighed. "She doesn't dwell on what might have been. She made her peace with that long ago and moved on. Better than the rest of us did, in some ways. Anyway, she'd been accepted into the American Ballet Theatre's Studio Company. Each year, twelve young dancers with outstanding potential are selected for the program."

As she refocused on the picture, her expression grew melancholy. "Being a professional ballerina was Cate's dream, and her dedication was absolute. While other young girls were going to parties or worrying about getting dates for the prom, Cate was dancing. Grueling hour after hour at the barre, with single-minded determination, always focused on her goal. And she was on her way to achieving it when she got sick. The illness itself was devastating, but after she got past the worst of it, we all assumed she'd recover. Except that wasn't in God's plan for our Cate. Sometimes I don't know how she…"

"Okay, I'm all set. Where are the…" Cate's words faltered as she came upon her mother and Clay standing by her photo. But she made a quick recovery. "I hope you're not boring Clay with ancient history, Mom." Her teasing tone was a bit forced, her smile a little too bright.

It might be old news to them, but there were a lot of questions Clay wanted answered. He opened his mouth to ask a few only to have Emily cut him off.

"Are you going to show us the pond now, Cate?"

"Yes. Let's go." She took the children's hands and started toward the door. "Coming, Clay?"

"Yeah. I'm right behind you."

As he followed in their wake, he recalled the day she'd told him about her illness. And how he'd tried to imagine what it would be like to be struck with such a debilitating condition just as the whole world was opening up before you. He'd wondered how it had changed Cate's life, what dreams she'd been forced to give up. But he'd had no idea of the magnitude of her loss. He couldn't begin to imagine how horrible it must be for someone once so active and agile to be unable to do a simple thing like fly a kite.

Instead of walking all the way to the attractive, stone-edged pond in the Shepard backyard, he lowered himself to a bench off to one side. As Cate pointed out the fish to the children, her father joined them, wiping his hands on a dish towel. The kids instantly became more subdued and pressed closer to Cate. But once her father talked with them and handed them some food to sprinkle on the water, they relaxed. Cate backed off, joining Clay on the bench.

"I asked Dad to come out and spend a few minutes one-on-one with the kids. I hope it will help them understand not all fathers are like theirs."

Clay was grateful for her concern for the children. But his thoughts remained on her. And he voiced the question that had come to his mind the day she'd first told him of her illness.

"How did you ever find the strength to cope?"

A few seconds of silence followed his quiet query as Cate watched the children. He wasn't sure she'd answer, but at last she lifted one shoulder. "It wasn't meant to be. God had other plans for me."

"Just like that? After all that study and sacrifice, you simply accepted that disaster as God's will?"

"No. It took me years to get to where I am now. In the beginning, I considered the illness a major setback, but not a career-ending catastrophe. I didn't give up the hope of recovery for a long, long time." She shrugged. "But in the end, I had to. And that's when the anger hit. I was furious with God. How could He do this to me, after the years of work I'd put into reaching my goal? I quit praying. I stopped going to church. I wanted nothing more to do with Him."

"That makes sense to me."

"It did to me, too. But in the end I realized that while I might have left God, He never left me. And as my anger subsided and I began to accept what had happened, I started to hear His voice again. I didn't always like what He was telling me, but I couldn't ignore it. That quote from Jeremiah kept replaying in my mind, about how God has plans for us, plans for our welfare, not our woe; plans to give us a future full of hope. After that, I began to open myself to His direction."

A faint smile touched her lips. "My life may not be the one I planned, Clay. But it's good. And it's the one God wants for me. Once I accepted that, I found peace."

Searching her eyes, Clay found nothing but sincerity in their depths. While her calm acceptance was hard for him to fathom, it nevertheless had an unexpected soothing effect on his troubled spirit. And it left him a tad envious; she'd found a peace he'd never discovered in all his years of restless wandering.

She tilted her head and regarded him. "Does my attitude surprise you?"

"Yes."

"Why?"

"I haven't been much of a churchgoer, Cate. But I've been listening to Reverend Richards for the past few weeks. And I have to admit I've been impressed. He paints a different picture of the Almighty than the one I was taught as a child. An appealing picture of a God of mercy and kindness. But God wasn't very kind or merciful to you."

"I didn't think so, either, at first. But I've come to believe there's a reason for what happened. And in His time, God will reveal it to me."

He shook his head. "I guess I'm just not sure why you have such great trust in God. I mean, I can tell all of you are very religious. But I grew up in a religious, God-fearing home, too. And I turned away from God."

"Ah." A smile whispered at her lips. "There's the difference. We grew up in a God-*loving* home—not a God-fearing one."

The comparison jolted him. In a few words, she'd captured the critical disparity in their upbringings, he realized. "You may be right. Fear was the operative word in our house."

She didn't press, didn't push, but he sensed she was receptive if he wanted to share more. He stared into the placid waters of the pond a dozen yards away, debating how much to reveal.

"My father considered himself to be a very religious man, but he was harsh and domineering. He always stressed the God of punishment, and he formulated an endless list of strict rules he claimed were based on the Good Book. Or his interpretation of it, anyway. He pretty much viewed the world through a black and white lens. There was no room for discussion, no tolerance of dissension. He held me and Anne and my mother to such impossible standards that we often failed to meet his expectations."

His inflection went flat. "There was no joy or warmth or love in our house. My mother tried to create some, but her efforts were thwarted by my father. And every week he'd drag us to these fire-and-brimstone Sunday services, where a preacher would rant and rave about what terrible sinners we were and how we were all going to hell if we didn't repent. My father took it all in, holier than thou, with his bible clutched to his chest." His last comment was riddled with bitterness.

"I can see why you wanted nothing to do with Christianity."

"Yeah, well, my father didn't see it that way." Clay gave a brief, mirthless laugh. "When I was fifteen, I'd had it. I rebelled and told him I wasn't going to church anymore. And I didn't. I think he wore out several belts on my back before he accepted the fact that nothing was going to change my mind."

"He beat you?" Shock rippled through her voice.

"He hit me." Clay gave a stiff shrug. "I'm not sure it would qualify as beating. And he was very self-righteous about it. Said he was doing it in the name of God for the good of my soul because he wanted me to be saved. I think he felt totally justified."

"Oh, Clay." Distress tightened her features. "I'm more sorry than I can say. No wonder you turned away from religion. The God I know would never justify the kind of behavior your father used in His name. Love works so much better than force if you want to touch people's hearts."

"I think you're right." Clay angled toward her, and the warmth in her eyes reached into the deepest recesses of his heart, like the spring sun coaxing new life from dormant plants. "Can I tell you something? You've given me a more favorable impression of religion in the past few minutes than any of those fire-and-brimstone preachers did in the first fourteen years of my life."

"Uncle Clay! Uncle Clay! Come see the red fish!"

It took Clay a moment to disengage from Cate's compelling

gaze. "I'll be right there, Josh." When he looked back at Cate she smiled.

"It's nice to be wanted."

"Yeah." But as he rose and headed for the pond, he couldn't help wishing he was also wanted by Cate.

Cate remained on the bench, watching as Clay dropped down to the children's level and engaged in an animated discussion. She needed a few minutes to mull over his startling revelations.

Given his father's example, it was no wonder he was a reluctant churchgoer. Nor was his insecurity about his child-rearing skills surprising. And his aversion to commitments also made sense. The relationships in his life had been dysfunctional, and he'd been badly hurt. Why would he want to take that risk again?

Each day since Clay and the children had come into her life, she'd asked the Lord to give him strength and wisdom to deal with the responsibilities he'd taken on. But now she added another request—for healing. Clay needed that as much as the children did. Without it, he'd never be able to open his heart to love or to the Lord's empowering grace. He would continue to exist on the fringes of life, unwilling—and afraid—to make a commitment to anyone. And that wasn't an ideal way to live.

Cate knew that firsthand, and would change her circumstances in a heartbeat if she could. She'd like nothing better than to be involved in a committed, caring relationship with a man she loved, surrounded by a houseful of children.

But in a culture that revered external beauty, where the quest for physical perfection bordered on the obsessive, it was hard for people to see beyond her obvious imperfections. Especially when it came to romance. Even the man she'd loved—a good, decent, faith-filled person—hadn't been able to look past them in the end.

Yet impediments of a different kind held Clay back, she mused, watching him reach out a gentle hand to steady Emily as she bent over the pond. While they might be less visible, in a sense they were as much a disability as hers.

And until he found a way to deal with them, there was little hope he'd achieve the kind of connections that would give him the peace she sensed he craved.

Chapter Six

Clay pulled into the parking space near his apartment, bone-weary after dealing with several days' worth of pressing problems at the job site. What he wanted was a long, cold drink and a quiet relaxing evening.

But when he glanced up to the landing, he found Cate waiting for him. That, in itself, was unusual. But some nuance in her posture also put him on alert.

So much for his quiet evening.

Taking the steps two at a time, he strode toward her. "Is everything okay?"

"Yes. I just wanted to talk to you, and there's not much privacy inside."

"Okay." He leaned back against the railing, his palms flat on the top, bracing for bad news.

"I thought we should revisit the bed-wetting situation." She pulled the sweater she'd thrown over her shoulders more tightly around her. "When you hired me, you said once it was under control you planned to put the children into a more traditional day care setting. Since the problem seems to be history, I thought we ought to discuss your plans. A friend of mine gave me a referral earlier this week for a child care position, and I need to consider it if you're planning to send the children to day care soon."

As Clay regarded Cate, he tried to regroup. It was true they'd agreed to a temporary arrangement. But he hadn't given a single thought to making any changes. The children were thriving under her attentive care. She was perfect for them.

Perfect.

The word suited her, he reflected, drinking in the sight of her in the afternoon light of this late April day. Ironic, too, considering the first thing he'd noticed about her had been her limp. Now he realized it was inconsequential. As was her disabled hand. They had no bearing on how he or the children felt about her. If she left, Josh and Emily would panic.

Sort of the same reaction he was already having.

He curled his fingers around the railing and held his breath. "I don't see any reason to change our arrangement at any time in the near future, if you're willing to stay."

Her soft lips curved into a smile that sent relief—and warmth—coursing through him. "I'm willing. I just wanted to be sure we were both on the same wavelength." She turned toward the door. "I need to tell the kids good-night before I leave."

For a few seconds, Clay remained outside. He was deeply grateful that Cate was willing to stay. Her presence in their lives was a natural fit, one he had come to accept—and expect.

Yet one of these days, she would go. Emily would start school next year, and Josh was right behind her. The kids wouldn't require a full-time nanny. Cate would have to move on to another family that needed her.

But it was getting harder and harder for Clay to envision a time when *this* family wouldn't need her.

Him included.

* * *

The sudden chime of the doorbell distracted Clay from the plans he was going over on the kitchen table. Odd. They never had visitors on Saturday. Unless Cate had stopped by for some reason. Now there was a pleasant thought, he mused, a smile tugging up the corners of his lips.

Stepping over the children, who were coloring on the floor in the living room, he reached down to tickle them. As they giggled and squirmed, he savored the feeling of contentment produced by their simple, uninhibited joy.

With a smile of welcome, Clay pulled open the door.

"Hello, boy. I've come for the children."

His smile evaporated. He hadn't seen his father in close to ten years, nor talked to him except for their one brief phone conversation after Anne died, and he almost didn't recognize him. He remembered his old man standing ramrod straight; now he looked shrunken and shriveled. His face was sallow and gaunt, his thinning hair gun-metal gray. But his eyes were as harsh and humorless as ever. That hadn't changed.

As Clay's shock receded, the man's words began to register. *I've come for the children.*

Clay felt like someone had kicked him in the gut.

All along, he'd known his father intended to take the children after he recovered. But he'd expected the man to call first to discuss the situation. And there was a lot to discuss. Because Clay didn't intend to send Josh and Emily to live with their grandfather. He hadn't yet figured out how he was going to permanently assimilate two little children into his life, but he'd assumed he'd have plenty of time to address that problem down the road.

He'd assumed wrong.

As he and his father faced off, Clay realized the room behind him had gone still as death. Checking on the kids over his shoulder, he found Josh and Emily huddled together, Emily's arm around Josh's shoulder in the familiar, protective gesture she hadn't used for weeks. They'd moved behind Clay, letting his body shield them from the intruder.

Clay clamped his lips into a thin, uncompromising line. "Let's talk outside."

The older man's eyes narrowed. "We don't have anything to talk about."

Turning his back on his father, Clay knelt beside the children. They looked at him with wide, anxious eyes while darting fearful glances at the figure in the doorway.

"I'm going to go outside and talk to your grandfather for a minute. After we're finished, why don't the three of us go get hamburgers and French fries? Would you like that?" He took Emily's hand, ruffled Josh's hair, keeping his touch and his voice gentle and reassuring.

Josh sniffled and edged closer to Emily. She tightened her grip on her brother's shoulder. Neither responded.

"Hey, it will be okay." He gathered them close and gave them a hug. "You guys go put on your shoes, and we'll head out in a few minutes. We might even stop for ice cream on the way home."

"Come on, Josh." Emily's sad, resigned tone tore at his heart as she tugged on her brother's hand.

Clay waited until they reached the hall before standing to face his father. Though he kept his volume low, the hostility came through loud and clear. "The kids are already upset. They don't need to hear this. Let's go outside."

He assumed his father would object. Instead, the older man gave the apartment a quick, disapproving scan and retreated to the landing. Clay followed, shutting the door behind them with a firm click. He stood in front of it and folded his arms across his chest.

"We're wasting time." The older man flicked an impatient hand toward the apartment. "Just pack up their things and we'll go."

"No."

Disbelief robbed his father of speech for an instant. "What?"

"I said no. I'm not sending the children to live with you."

"You can't be serious. You're not equipped to deal with two children."

"And you are?"

"I raised two of my own."

"And you did such a superb job." Sarcasm dripped off Clay's words.

The older man bristled. "Who are you to judge me?"

"And who are you to judge me?" Clay countered, his voice taut.

His father snorted. "I know what kind of life you lead, boy. Always on the move, living in tiny apartments not fit for a family, probably a girl in every port. A Godless life. That's an inappropriate environment for children."

"You don't know a thing about the life I lead." Clay bit out the words, struggling to hold on to his temper.

"I know enough. You're nothing like Anne. She was a good girl who always did what she was supposed to do."

"Yeah. And she ended up dead. Thanks to you."

His father's complexion went a shade sallower. "That's a terrible thing to say!"

"It's the truth. If you hadn't pressured her to stay in that farce of a marriage, she'd be alive today."

The last of the color drained from the older man's face. "You always did have a smart mouth. I'm surprised you didn't get into trouble in the Army."

"I did fine in the Army. I respected the authority *there*. And I'm doing fine now. I don't need you. Nor do Josh and Emily. You did enough damage to your own children. I'm not letting you do the same to these two."

"And how are you going to stop me?"

"I have them. You don't."

"I'm their grandfather."

"I'm their uncle."

The older man glared at him, his fury daunting. But Clay didn't flinch. And he didn't move from the door.

At last Clay's father reached into his pocket and withdrew his car keys, ending the standoff. "I'm not finished with you yet, boy."

Though a tremor of fear ran through him, Clay did his best to appear impassive as he regarded the man in silence.

Clearly frustrated, his father turned away. But as Clay watched him retreat toward his car, his shoulders stiff, he had a sinking feeling that while he might have won this battle, the war was just beginning.

"Thank you for doing this, Cate. I'm sorry to bother you on a Saturday, but I'm in over my head. Again. I knew you'd handle this better than I would."

Pulling her condo door shut behind her, Cate cast a worried look at Clay's haggard face, noting the fine lines etched at the corners of his mouth, the faint shadows beneath his eyes. His compliment warmed her, but she wasn't sure it was deserved. Not yet, anyway. She was good with children, but a visit from a near stranger who was threatening their shaky sense of security could wreak havoc with Emily and Josh, undoing all the good she and Clay had accomplished over the past six weeks. "It's not a bother. How are the children?"

"Quiet. Too quiet." He glanced toward the car, distress carving deeper grooves on either side of his mouth.

"We need to get them to talk about today. But first let's just work on getting them to talk."

As they drove to the fast-food outlet, Cate did her best to engage the children in conversation. But despite her diligent efforts, the best she was able to get was monosyllable responses from Emily and silence from Josh. The two of them sat slumped in their car seats, holding hands. Emily stared out the window and Josh stuck his thumb in his mouth.

Not good, Cate concluded as Clay pulled into a parking spot. And the man beside her wasn't in much better shape. Anger shimmered off him, and the grim set of his lips was rigid as granite.

"Sit tight, guys. Uncle Clay and I will unbuckle you." Cate motioned for Clay to get out of the truck. Easing to the ground, she moved forward to speak to him over the hood, keeping her voice low. "I know you're as upset as they are. But children pick up tension, and your anger is only going to make this worse. If you want to take five minutes alone and try to chill out a little, I can watch the kids."

He sucked in a deep breath. "Okay. Can you get them out of the truck?"

"Yes. Don't worry. We'll be fine."

Ten minutes later, when Clay slid into the booth where Cate and the children sat, he was loaded down with food and appeared far less tense, Cate noted with relief.

During the meal, he did his best to engage the children in small talk, following her lead. He managed a joke or two, teased Emily about her milk mustache, and tousled Josh's hair twice.

But nothing worked. Both of the children picked at their food. Even their fries were hardly touched.

After it was clear they'd eaten as much as they were going to, Cate and Clay gathered up the remains of the lunch. As Clay slipped back into the booth after disposing of the trash, arching an eyebrow in her direction, she laid her hands on the table, palms up. "Let's all hold hands for a minute, okay?" Signaling to Clay, she wiggled the fingers of one hand in his direction and extended her other hand toward Emily, who sat beside her.

Clay immediately enfolded her fingers in his. Despite the serious nature of this tête-à-tête, his strong, sure touch played havoc with her metabolism. But this wasn't about her. Or them, she reminded herself. This was about helping the children. She needed to focus.

And Emily's hand creeping into hers helped her do that.

Smiling down at the little girl, Cate gave her an encouraging squeeze. Josh had taken Clay's hand, too, and the children also reached across the table and linked fingers. The four pairs of hands formed a lopsided circle on the Formica top.

"That's better, isn't it? It always makes me happy to hold hands with people I love." Cate said the last word without thinking, and her cheeks grew warm. Risking a quick peek in Clay's direction, she couldn't tell if the emotion in his eyes was residual anger—or something different but equally powerful.

Fixing her gaze on the children, Cate focused on them. "It's also easier to talk about things you're worried about if you hold hands. Uncle Clay told me your grandfather came to visit today. Are you worried about that?"

A sniffle preceded Emily's answer. "Do we have to go with him?" Her question came out in a tremulous whisper.

Though Cate was far better at dealing with situations like this than he was, Clay knew it wasn't fair to let her handle the tough questions. So he stepped in, doing his best to imitate her gentle, encouraging inflection. "I'm going to do everything I can to make sure you don't. I want you to stay with me. Would you like that?"

"Yes. We don't like him. He's scary," Emily responded.

Clay could empathize, but he wanted to hear their version. "How come?"

"He used to come and visit sometimes. But he wasn't very nice. And he never smiled. He told me if I wasn't a good girl, I'd go to hell."

"He said in hell, people burn. I don't want to burn." Josh's words quavered as he added his recollections.

Once more, Clay's fury escalated. To instill fear into two innocent children too young to know the meaning of the word *bad* was no less than criminal. But Cate's gentle warning squeeze of his fingers helped him stifle his anger as he struggled to maintain a placid expression.

"You aren't going to go to hell, Josh," Clay assured him. "And you aren't going to go to live with your grandfather, either, if I can help it."

"But what if he comes b-back?" Emily's voice caught on the last word.

Based on his father's parting words, Clay suspected that was a probable scenario. But he didn't plan to let the old man have the children. Period.

"You live with me," he told Josh and Emily in a firm tone. "And your grandfather lives far away. You don't need to worry about him coming back very often. If he does, I'll be here to keep you safe."

It was a promise Clay intended to keep, and he said it with sufficient conviction to ease the children's tension.

"We like it here with you," Josh told him, and Emily bobbed her head. "It's the bestest place we've ever lived."

Clay tried to swallow past the lump in his throat. "It's the bestest place I ever lived, too."

And that was no lie. Though he'd traveled all over the world, lived in exotic lands and in a dozen cities across the United States, he'd always been alone. Having these two children—and the warm, caring woman across from him—in his life had made even his tiny apartment feel like a real home.

As they walked toward his truck a few minutes later holding hands, the children tucked between him and Cate, he vowed to do everything he could to restore to their lives the fragile peace and security they'd just begun to enjoy.

But it wasn't going to be easy, not with the looming threat from his father. And while he'd tried to reassure them, he knew the children were aware of the danger.

Because that night, for the first time in weeks, Josh had an accident.

Two weeks later, when Clay noted the caller ID on his office phone, his pulse ratcheted up. Cate had never called him at work before.

Grabbing the receiver, he locked it against his ear.

"Cate?" Despite his efforts to remain calm, alarm nipped at his voice.

"A letter arrived for you today from a Des Moines law firm."

"Where are the kids?"

"Inside, eating lunch. I'm on the landing."

"Okay. Go ahead and open it. No sense putting off bad news."

The sound of rustling paper came over the line, followed by silence that seemed to last forever. "It's written in typical incomprehensible legalese," Cate said at last. "But the gist is clear. Your father is appealing to the court for custody, claiming you're an unfit guardian."

Clay uttered a word that made her gasp.

"Sorry." He expelled a frustrated breath. "I was afraid this was going to happen. But I guess I was hoping he'd let it go."

"There's also some stuff in here about your lifestyle that's not very…pretty."

"I can imagine." Coiled anger stiffened his words. "My father always thought I led a wild, wanton life."

"Yeah. It kind of suggests that."

At her faint response, his stomach clenched. Tightening his grip on the phone, he massaged his temples with his free hand. "Cate, I don't know what's in there. But I can promise you it's greatly exaggerated."

"They can make an issue of it, though, in court. If this gets that far."

Clay closed his eyes. The last thing he wanted to do was drag the kids through a court battle. But he couldn't let them fall into the hands of his father, either. "I hope it doesn't come to that."

"I'm no legal expert, but the stuff in here sounds pretty serious. I think you're going to need an attorney. I'm sure Mark would be willing to help you out."

Though he hadn't had a chance to talk much to Cate's brother at Easter dinner, the man had struck him as sharp and insightful. "Good idea. I'll give him a call." Sighing, he wiped a hand down his face and regarded the defective blueprint on his desk. Problems at work, problems at home. Could things get any more complicated?

"Hey." Cate's gentle, sympathetic voice interrupted his pity party. "Things will work out."

"I wish I had your confidence."

In truth, what he wished was that she was sitting beside him now, their fingers entwined. Those few minutes a couple of weeks ago, as they'd held hands at the fast-food restaurant, had been an oasis of comfort and calm in the chaos that had become his life. And for a man who had always thought he operated best alone, that brief physical connection had been an eye-opening example of the power of sharing and unity.

"When people are committed to doing the right thing, the Lord can work wonders, Clay." Cate's earnest encouragement came over the line, instilling a spark of hope. "And no matter what challenges come up, we'll address them."

We'll address them.

Knowing Cate had taken on his fight as if it were her own did more to uplift his spirits than anything else. "I'll keep that in mind."

And as he hung up, Clay resolved that he would win the battle brewing with his father.

No matter what it took.

Chapter Seven

The next morning, Mark set a yellow legal pad on the mahogany conference table in his office and took a seat opposite Clay. "I reviewed the document you couriered over. And I have a few questions."

"I figured you would."

"You may not like some of them."

"I don't like any of this."

"It's only going to get messier." Mark picked up a pen and settled back in his chair. "Tell me about your father."

Clay gave a derisive snort. "He's a joyless, authoritarian tyrant with a twisted view of Christianity who leaves misery in his wake."

Mark tapped his pen against the palm of his hand. "I'm picking up a lot of hate here."

"Yeah, well, I don't exactly harbor good feelings about the old man. And he's ill-equipped to raise Josh and Emily."

"In your opinion."

Leaning forward, Clay gripped the edge of the table. "It's not opinion. I lived with that man. I *know* what it's like. I wouldn't wish that kind of childhood on my worst enemy."

Mark regarded Clay with a dispassionate expression. "The court will consider facts, not feelings or conjecture. So let's examine the facts." He scanned the document Clay had received from his father's attorney. "Your father claims you have no stable home in which to raise the children. Is that true?"

"It depends on how you define stable."

"How long have you lived at your present address?"

"About three months."

"Where did you live before that?"

"Indianapolis."

"For how long?"

"Eight months."

"And before that?"

"Cleveland. For sixteen months."

"And your father lives in Des Moines. Does he have a house?"

"Yes."

"How long has he lived there?"

Clay gritted his teeth. "Forty years. Okay, I get your point."

"Good. But there's more. Do you attend church on a regular basis?"

"I do now."

"Since when?"

"Since I got the kids."

"How about your father?"

"He's gone every week for as long as I can remember. But that doesn't mean he's a good Christian."

"We're only looking at facts, remember? What are your finances like?"

"I do okay."

"Would you say you're as well off as your father? Able to provide the children with as many material advantages as he can?"

"I can give them everything they need."

"You didn't answer my question."

"Okay." Clay's breath hissed out through his teeth. "From a financial perspective, my father has the resources to give them a more cushy life. But he won't."

"Prove it."

A cold knot of fear twisted Clay's stomach. "This isn't looking good, is it?"

"It's not a lost cause. But I want you to know what you're going to be up against if this goes before a judge. Let's talk for a minute about your father's claim that you lead a 'wild' life."

"That's a bunch of…nonsense." Clay changed his choice of noun at the last second.

Mark eyed him. "You're…how old, Clay?"

"Thirty-four."

"And single."

"You make that sound like a sin."

"Depends on the reason. There are implications in this document that in terms of morality, you're a bit on the shall we say, liberal side. Not the best environment for children."

"I would never do anything to hurt the children. But I'm not into the commitment thing, either. And marriage is a big commitment."

"So is raising two kids." A few beats of silence ticked by as Mark regarded him. "Is there anything in your life a private investigator could uncover that would hurt your case?"

Clay stared at him. He'd never considered the possibility his father would hire someone to dig for dirt. But he wouldn't put it past the old man. "I don't think so. I was in the service for twelve years. I've been employed ever since. I've never had any trouble with the law."

"I know. I already checked all that out. Just like the other side will," Mark added, forestalling Clay's protest. "Let's talk about the picture that's emerging."

"I think I already have a pretty good idea." Clay wondered if he looked as bleak as he felt.

"Let me lay it out for you, anyway. Your father's attorney will point to the rootless nature of your job and claim you're a drifter of questionable moral character, with no solid religious affiliations and far fewer financial resources than the children's grandfather. Your father, on the other hand, will be portrayed as a churchgoing pillar of the community, with a stable home, solid moral character, significant financial resources and experience in raising children and creating a home."

"Those may appear to be the facts, but they couldn't be further from the truth." Clay raked his fingers through his hair. "So where do we go from here?"

"We fight them."

Clay gave him a skeptical look. "You think we have a chance of winning?"

"That depends on you. How serious you are about keeping the children?"

"Very."

"Enough to make some significant changes in your life?"

Clay swallowed hard. "Yes."

"Then we may have a chance. First of all, possession is nine-tenths of the law. You're a family member, and you have the children. The court won't take them away without cause before a hearing. And they're not going to find one. I saw the children at Easter. It's obvious they're well-cared for and happy. But now that these papers have been filed, you'll be checked out."

"How?"

"Expect some visits from a social worker. They'll be unannounced. The intent is to catch you and the children in your daily routine."

"Okay."

"Now let's talk about changes. The court is not going to be disposed in your favor if you're moving every few months. You're going to need to think about a job that lets you stay in one place. Are you willing to consider that?"

Although Clay liked his work, he had no particular loyalty to his firm. It was a job, nothing more. And there were other, less mobile jobs for people with his skills and experience. "Yes."

"Good. How large is your apartment?"

"Tiny. It's an efficiency. I had it before I got the kids."

"Move. To a house, if you can manage it. Renting is fine, but the court always prefers houses to apartments. It's more important in this case, considering your father is offering a house. If we can demonstrate your willingness to make these kinds of changes for the good of the children, we'll have a stronger case."

"I guess it would help if I had a wife, too, wouldn't it?" Clay's mouth twisted into a humorless smile.

"No question about it. Do you have someone in mind?" When Clay did a double take, Mark flashed him a smile. "Just kidding. I don't think you have to go that far. After all, your father is only offering a single-parent household, too."

"So what do I do next?"

"Wait for the social worker to visit. Rent a house. Start putting out feelers for a different job." Mark rose and held out his hand. "I'll be in touch."

Clay's head was spinning as he returned the man's firm clasp. "This isn't going to be easy, is it?"

Tucking his pen into the pocket of his jacket, Mark gave him a steady look. "Most things worth fighting for aren't."

Cate was waiting at the door when Clay walked into the apartment that night. She'd hoped the meeting with Mark had gone well, but the weary droop of Clay's shoulders wasn't encouraging.

"What did he say?"

Dropping a roll of blueprints on the couch, Clay checked over her shoulder. "Where are the kids?"

"In the bedroom. Playing an educational video game on your old laptop."

He let out a long, slow, breath. "Your brother is one tough interrogator."

A wry smile tugged at her lips. "He's always been like that. You should have heard him giving my boyfriends the third degree when I was in high school. And his technique has only improved with age."

Clay's mouth twitched. "All I can say is, I'd hate to be on a witness stand with him asking the questions. Let's sit for a minute."

She moved to the couch and he perched on the chair, the muscles in his shoulders bunching as he leaned forward to clasp his hands. After giving her a quick recap, he shook his head. "I'm willing to do everything he suggested, but I'm not sure it will be enough."

"It has to be. I can't believe anyone would send those children to the kind of environment you describe. Not after all the sacrifices you're making to do what's best for them."

"That's the odd thing." He shook his head and raked his fingers through his hair. "I don't feel as if I'm making any sacrifice at all. I feel as if I'm getting way more out of this deal than they are."

Cate smiled. "It's amazing how two little kids can worm their way into your heart, isn't it?"

"The kids aren't the only ones who've managed to do that."

At his unexpected comment, Cate's smile fled. And as their gazes locked, what she saw in his dark eyes rocked her world.

It was attraction, pure and simple. More potent and powerful than anything she'd ever seen in the eyes of the man she once loved.

The silence between them began to pulse with a tension that had nothing to do with the custody issue. And it intensified when Clay reached over and took her hand.

Cate stopped breathing.

From the beginning, she'd felt a strong pull toward this man. And it seemed the feeling was mutual. But she suspected Clay's attraction was based on appreciation. She'd bailed him out several times with the kids, and he was grateful. Gratitude had led to liking. But those didn't add up to an attraction that lasted. To love. They added up to a recipe for hurt. She'd been on the receiving end of feelings masquerading as love once. And she had no desire to repeat the experience.

Summoning up every ounce of her willpower, Cate pulled her hand away with a gentle tug. "I need to check on the children."

To her relief, he let her go. Perhaps he was already regretting his impulsive gesture, she speculated.

But when she took a quick peek at him before ducking into the hall, his expression was pensive rather than chagrined or embarrassed. As if he was trying to figure out why she'd retreated—or was planning his next move.

Both of which made her decidedly uncomfortable.

A week later, a plaintive wail pierced the night, yanking Clay back from the brink of sleep.

It was Emily. Again.

Adrenaline pumping, he swung his feet to the floor and

covered the distance to the children's bedroom in a few long strides. She was thrashing on the bed, in the throes of a nightmare. A bad one.

Josh, on the other hand, remained sound asleep, oblivious to his sister's distress. The kid could sleep through anything, Clay marveled, shaking his head as he leaned over to brush the hair back from Emily's flushed cheeks. "It's okay, Emily. You're okay," he soothed.

Although he kept repeating that mantra, it had little effect. Recalling how she'd clung to him during the daylight episode, he picked her up and cradled her in his arms, hoping that would help.

But when her whole body began to twitch and she clutched at him convulsively, his panic escalated. The first time Emily had had a meltdown, Cate had come to his rescue. But he was on his own tonight. And he had no idea what to do.

Maybe he should sit on the couch, he reasoned, heading toward the living room. That had worked before. Except then, Emily had been awake and gripping his neck, not asleep and writhing in his arms. This was a different scenario.

He sat and tried rocking her, murmuring comforting words, but that seemed to agitate her more—until all at once she began to mutter and fight against him, exhibiting amazing strength for such a tiny thing.

Realizing he was getting nowhere, Clay gave her a gentle shake, trying to awaken her. It took several attempts, each a bit more vigorous, but at last she awoke with a gasp, her eyes wild, her body rigid.

"Emily, it's okay." Clay said the words slowly, in a gentle tone, "You're safe. You're with Uncle Clay. You just had a nightmare."

He stroked her back, emulating the rhythmic motion Cate had

used during the last episode, until at last her body went limp and she collapsed against him, sobbing.

"I—I was afraid he was going to h-hurt her." Emily hiccupped, gulping air.

"It was a bad dream, honey. It's over now." A shudder rippled through her, and he tightened his grasp. "Everything's okay now."

"It—it wasn't her fault." She continued as if he hadn't spoken.

"I know. Your mommy didn't do anything wrong."

"No." She gave her head an emphatic shake. "M-my dream wasn't about Mommy. It was about Cate."

Shock rippled through Clay, and he backed off a fraction to scrutinize Emily's face. "Are you sure you were dreaming about Cate?"

"Yes. It was about the mean man who yelled at her in the parking lot today. He looked really mad. I—I was afraid he was going t-to hit her."

Clueless, Clay tried to make sense of Emily's story. Cate hadn't mentioned anything unusual about the day. She'd told him she'd spent most of it packing for the move to the small house he'd rented. But then again, she hadn't talked a whole lot to him since the day he'd taken her hand while she sat on this very couch. She'd been skittish in his presence, and she no longer lingered in the evening to exchange news of the day, as she once had.

"Are you sure this really happened, Emily?" Clay probed.

"Yes. At the grocery store. The cart started to roll away and it almost hit that man's car. Cate stopped it, but he got mad anyway. It wasn't her fault."

The story was credible enough to merit checking out, Clay decided. But first he needed to calm Emily's fears.

"I'm sure it wasn't, honey. And everything's fine now. Didn't you come home after that and bake cookies?" He managed a smile as he touched the tip of her nose.

"Uh huh. Oatmeal." She sniffled and gripped his hand. "That man made me think about D-Daddy. He's not coming back, is he?"

"No, Emily, he's not. He won't ever bother you again." Clay had been in regular touch with the Omaha police department. They'd found the man's abandoned car a few days after he'd disappeared, the children's car seats still in place, but they'd had no luck yet tracking him down. Once they did find him, however, he'd be thrown into a hole for the rest of his life. And he could rot there, as far as Clay was concerned.

Reassured, Emily relaxed against him. "I like you as a daddy much better."

Warmth flooded Clay's heart as he stood to carry her back to the bedroom. And when she wrapped her thin arms around his neck, the same protective instinct he'd once felt for Anne came bubbling to the surface. A lump rose in his throat as he recalled his sweet, gentle sister. From the time she was a little girl, he'd wanted to shield her from harm's way, to keep her safe.

In the end, he'd failed her.

But he didn't intend to fail her children.

The ringing of the phone pulled Cate out of a deep sleep, and she squinted at the clock, trying to focus. Eleven-fifteen. Not good. Late calls meant emergencies.

She checked her caller ID, and her pulse went into a staccato beat as she snatched the phone from her nightstand. "Clay? What's wrong?"

"I'm sorry to bother you at this hour. Were you asleep?"

"It doesn't matter. What's wrong?"

"Emily had another meltdown. A nightmare this time."

Struggling to a sitting position, Cate pushed her hair back from her face. "Is she okay?"

"Yeah. I got her settled and put back to bed."

"Okay. Good." Cate took a deep breath and leaned back against the headboard. "Don't be too concerned, Clay. Considering all they've been through, I'm surprised they haven't both had more problems with nightmares. The memories of their volatile situation at home are imbedded in their subconscious. They're bound to come through in dreams now and then."

"This nightmare wasn't about their former life. It was about you. That's why I called. She said there was some kind of incident today at the grocery store?"

Surprise arched Cate's eyebrows. "I knew she was upset, but I thought we'd gotten past that."

"What happened?"

"It was no big deal. I lost control of the cart for a moment. A passing motorist was more than a little peeved when it came within inches of his very expensive car, and he let me know that in no uncertain terms. Emily witnessed it, but Josh was already in the car."

"The guy didn't threaten you, did he?"

The quiet menace in his question took her by surprise. He sounded as if he'd punch the guy out, given the chance. "No. I'm fine, Clay. There was never any danger."

"Okay." He expelled a breath. "Sorry I bothered you."

"It was no bother. I appreciate your concern."

A few seconds of silence ticked by. Outside Cate's open window, a distant rumble of thunder vibrated through the air, signaling the approach of unsettled weather.

Clay cleared his throat. "Look, Cate, about the other day— the hand thing. I've been trying to find an opportunity to bring it up, but you're always with the kids. Anyway, I know it made you uncomfortable, and I wanted to apologize for that. I'd like to get things between us back to where they were before. If that means hands off for now, so be it. I've got plenty of distractions anyway, with a custody battle looming. But the truth is, I like you—a lot. And once the situation with Josh and Emily is resolved, we need to talk."

She should have known he'd bring up their relationship eventually, Cate reflected in dismay. Clay was a forthright man who went after what he wanted with single-minded determination, no matter the obstacles. His custody fight was a good example of that.

But he'd been honest from the beginning about his aversion to committed relationships, and he'd already taken on more of those than he'd ever planned. He didn't need another one. Besides, she wasn't in the market for romance. Those were formidable hurdles even a tenacious man like Clay would have a hard time overcoming.

"There isn't anything to talk about, Clay."

"Sorry. I don't buy that. I'm not the playboy my father paints me to be, but I've dated my share of women. And unless my instincts are way off base, I think you're as interested in me as I am in you."

"Interest and inclination are two different things."

She could hear the frown in his voice when he responded. "You want to explain that?"

"Look, you have enough on your plate right now with the custody fight, okay? Don't look for more problems."

"I don't consider you a problem."

"That's a mistake. Trust me." The thunder rumbled again, closer now, and she forged ahead without giving him the opportunity to refute her statement. "Besides, we're very different people who want different things out of life."

"I'm not sure that's as true as it once was."

"I'm not willing to take that risk, Clay."

The silence on the line confirmed her suspicion that he was still not comfortable with the notion of commitment. While his willingness to assume responsibility for the children was a good sign, it didn't mean he was ready to pledge his life to a woman. Even if there were no other impediments to exploring a relationship, Clay's unsettled existence and uncertain future were major red flags.

But her experience with her ex-boyfriend was also a reason for her to step back. She'd come to believe he cared for her despite her disability, too. And she didn't intend to make that mistake again.

"I get your message, Cate." Clay interrupted her thoughts, his tone troubled. "And I don't blame you for your caution, given the situation. I'll tell you what. Why don't we table a discussion of personal matters until the custody issue is settled? That will give us both a chance to think things through and give me time to get my act together."

A flash of lightning illuminated the dark sky outside her window, turning night into day as it bathed the world in brilliance. But the burst of brightness didn't last.

Just like her experience of love, Cate thought with a bittersweet pang.

"All I'm asking for is some time, Cate."

At Clay's husky plea, she closed her eyes, squeezing back the sudden tears that clouded her vision—and her judgment. She shouldn't give him false hope. Her mind was clear on that particular point. But her heart refused to listen.

"Okay. Let's let it rest for a while."

"I'm good with that." The relief in his voice was palpable. "Now get some sleep."

But as the line went dead, Cate knew that was a lost cause.

Chapter Eight

"What the..." Clay turned into the driveway of the two-bedroom house he'd rented after his consultation with Mark two weeks ago and surveyed the scene.

Cate had offered to meet him here this morning to help unpack and get the children settled, so he'd expected to find her waiting for him on this balmy late-May Saturday. But he hadn't expected to find her father cutting the grass. Or Mark, up in the big oak tree out back, hanging a swing as Michelle directed his efforts from below. Or her mother setting out a picnic lunch on a portable table. Or Pop filling a neglected planter with flowers. Or Rob repairing the broken gate that led to the back yard.

The entire Shepard clan had shown up to help him move in.

He was dumfounded.

"There's Pop!" Josh exclaimed. "Hi, Pop!" he called through the open truck window, his vigorous wave communicating his excitement.

The older man smiled and waved back as Cate stepped out the front door. Her hair was pulled back into a ponytail, the simple style revealing the classic planes of her face and reminding Clay of the *Swan Lake* picture. She was dressed in blue-jean shorts and an oversized T-shirt and was carrying a mop.

As Clay set the brake, Rob swung open the back door of the extended cab and reached up to help the children out.

"Morning, Clay." He grinned and gave a thumbs up. "Nice house. The kids will love it."

"Thanks."

As he opened his own door and stepped down, Cate joined him, her green eyes sparking with excitement. "Surprise!"

"I'll say. What's going on?"

"Everyone wanted to help."

"Why?"

She tilted her head. "Moving isn't easy. And many hands make light work, as they say."

"But they hardly know me."

"The good Samaritan didn't know the injured stranger, either. Helping those in need is the Christian thing to do. My family has always been like this. When I was sick, they were constantly around."

He raked his fingers through his hair. "But didn't you sometimes feel like you were being…smothered…by all that attention?"

"No. I felt loved." She regarded him in silence for a moment, and when she continued her tone was more subdued. "I can ask everyone to finish up and head out if this is too much of a crowd for you."

Planting his fists on his hips, Clay tried to assess his reaction. Why was he unsettled by Cate's family turning out to lend a hand? After all, he needed all the help he could get. He should be grateful. Yet for some reason the scene created an anxious knot in the pit of his stomach.

"No. It's okay. I must sound like an ingrate."

"My family *can* be a little overwhelming." Cate shoved her hands into the pockets of her shorts and took a step back. "Come on inside. Mom and I have the place pretty spic and span already."

Leaving him by the truck, she headed for the front door.

As he trailed behind her, trying to decipher his uneasy reaction to the Shepards' generosity, a conversation he overhead as he passed Pop filling the planter with seedlings gave him his answer.

"Why are they wilted?" Josh asked.

"Because they've been moved too much." Pop carefully tucked a small plant into the soil. "Flowers need to stay in one place and be tended by someone who loves them. Then the roots spread out and grow strong, and they can withstand any storm that comes along."

All his life, Clay had thought of roots as chains. Pop saw them as an anchor, as a positive force that protected and nurtured and strengthened. Without roots, flowers wilted and shriveled and died.

It was a whole different concept of roots.

And he had to admit it held a certain appeal.

But it was also scary.

Yet whether he wanted them or not, Clay had roots now, thanks to the children. As Mark had pointed out, if he hoped to convince the court he was a fit guardian he was going to have to settle in one place. And once you did that, you began to form relationships. With neighbors. With coworkers. With church members.

Perhaps even with a special woman.

And those relationships brought responsibilities. Obligations. Risk.

Pain.

That's why he was uncomfortable with today's scenario, he concluded. It implied belonging. Connections. Closeness. All the things that reeked of commitment.

He'd done a good job avoiding that for his entire adult life. But things had changed when two little children had been thrust into his hands and stolen his heart. When a lovely woman had slipped into his life and forced him to rethink his long-held notions about commitments. When he'd started attending church and been exposed to a loving God who, he was told, wanted a relationship with him. And when a simple meal with Cate's family had drawn him into their fold.

That's why he was anxious.

All of those relationships were beginning to undermine his resolve to keep his distance.

And there didn't seem to be a thing he could do to shore it up.

Clay had finished collecting the dirty clothes and was weaving his way toward the washing machine through the boxes of new dishes and still-to-be-unpacked personal items when a startled cry of pain filtered in through the open window.

Josh.

Dropping the clothes in the middle of the living room, Clay took off at a sprint. It wasn't even nine o'clock in the morning, and they'd only been in the house a week. Already the toilet had overflowed; a backed-up gutter had sent a sheet of water cascading down the front window—which leaked; and the microwave had died. Now what?

As Clay closed the distance between him and the children, his pulse skyrocketed. Josh was sitting on the ground, crying. Emily was hovering beside him. And there was blood on Josh's face.

Lots of blood.

Clay dropped to the ground beside the children, and Emily looked at him tearfully. "Josh f-falled off the swing."

Taking his handkerchief out of his pocket, Clay lifted the

little boy's chin with a gentle finger, struggling to control his panic. "Let me see, Josh."

It didn't take him long to discover the source of the blood— a nasty gash an inch-and-a-half long on the youngster's chin that would need stitches.

After pressing his handkerchief to the cut, Clay gave the boy a quick but thorough scrutiny, gently probing his scalp. "Does anything else hurt, Josh?"

"N-no."

"Okay." Clay gathered him in his arms and ushered the children toward his truck. "We're going to have to let the doctor fix you up."

Josh's chin quivered. "Can Cate come?"

Both children gave him a hopeful look.

He wished she could. If she was with them, the kids would be calmer during the ordeal to come. And so would he. But he was doing his best not to call her on weekends. "This is her day off, Josh."

"Off from what?"

Good question. As far as the kids were concerned, she was part of their family, not a paid day care provider. And he was beginning to think of her that way, too.

"She has to have some time to do things for herself," Clay replied, avoiding the question. "I'll tell you what. After we're done, why don't we go out for hamburgers and French fries?" The fast-food treat was becoming his fallback after difficult situations, Clay realized. But, hey, whatever worked.

"Okay, I guess. But it would be better if Cate came."

Clay could only agree.

Four hours later—after an interminable wait in the emergency room; after ten gut-clenching minutes while Josh clung to his hand, whimpering in fear and pain as the doctor numbed his chin and put in a neat row of six stitches; and after enduring half an hour in a fast-foot outlet populated by noisy, hyperactive children—Clay pulled into their driveway, feeling more weary and overwhelmed than he had since the long, dark, solitary ride to Omaha for Anne's funeral.

He set the brake and checked on the children. Josh's head was drooping, and Emily was struggling to keep her eyes open. They all needed a nap after their trying morning. The laundry and grass-cutting could wait.

As Clay fitted the key in the lock and stepped inside, the aroma of burnt— or worse, burning—food greeted him. The lasagna, he concluded. Cate had made it last week, and with the microwave out of commission, she'd left instructions to heat three portions at a low temperature in the oven. He'd put it in shortly before Josh's accident and forgotten about it in the ensuing rush to the hospital.

After easing Josh onto the couch, he wove through the booby-trapped living room and headed toward the kitchen At least there wasn't any smoke, he noted in relief. But the smell was more pronounced in here.

Grabbing a towel, he opened the oven door.

Now he had smoke. Plenty of it. A billow surged out, and he waved the towel at it as the smoke alarm went off. Clay ignored the piercing whistle and pulled the lasagna from the oven, coughing as he deposited it on the counter and lifted a corner of the foil to peek in.

From the charred mess inside, it was obvious something had gone very wrong.

Leaving the smoldering pan on the counter, he retrieved Cate's instructions. Her neat script said to heat the lasagna at two hundred and fifty degrees for several hours. That was what he'd done. Wasn't it?

A quick check of the dial on the oven told him otherwise. With a sinking feeling, he saw that he'd misread the worn knob and set it at four hundred and fifty.

He was still flapping a towel at the raucous smoke alarm when Emily tugged urgently at his sleeve.

"There's somebody at the door," she shouted at him.

"Okay." As the smoke alarm fell silent, he wiped his forehead with his bloody handkerchief and picked his way through the living room. Josh was sprawled on the couch, sound asleep, his complexion pale beneath the large, unwieldy gauze pad the nurse had taped to his jaw. Clay shook his head. Amazing.

Emily hung back as he opened the door to reveal a middle-aged woman dressed in a tailored, navy blue suit. Her gaze dropped to the bloody handkerchief in his hand, and he stuffed it back into his pocket as his neck grew warm.

"Mr. Adams?"

"Yes."

"I'm Martha Douglas from the Division of Family Services. I've here for a home visit."

Several beats of silence ticked by as he stared at her. This had to be an episode from *The Twilight Zone.*

But no. The woman on the other side of the door was all too real.

His first instinct was to shut the door in her face—a reaction he quashed at once. That would do nothing to help his case.

Yet neither would the scene on the other side of the door.

He was wedged between the proverbial rock and a hard place. Faced with two bad options, there was only one possible choice. He forced himself to swing the door open.

"Come in, Ms. Douglas. We've had a rather trying morning.

Josh fell off the swing and cut his chin. We spent four hours in the emergency room, and the kids are pretty worn out."

Instead of responding, or offering the reassurance he was hoping for, the woman simply stepped inside. She smiled at the little girl hovering behind Clay.

"You must be Emily."

Emily gave Clay an uncertain look, and he somehow managed to force his lips into the semblance of a smile. "This is Ms. Douglas. She came to visit for a little while. Say hello."

"Hello," Emily parroted in a soft voice.

"That's a very pretty shirt," the woman told her. "Pink is one of my favorite colors."

"I brought this from Omaha."

"Omaha is a nice place."

"I like it better here."

Clay let out the breath he was holding. *Thank you, God!*

"Washington is nice, too. Is that your brother over there?" She gestured toward the couch, which had been delivered yesterday and was still covered in plastic. Josh continued to sleep.

"Yes. He falled off the swing and cut his chin."

"I see that. Have you had lunch yet?"

"Uh huh. We got hamburgers and French fries. And I had a milkshake." She named the fast-food outlet.

Clay cringed. Not good.

"I figured they deserved a treat after the morning we had," he offered. "We don't eat fast food, as a rule."

"Do you cook, Mr. Adams?" The woman's expression was placid and unreadable.

"A little. The woman who cares for the children shops for me and often makes casseroles for us. I'm afraid I burnt her lasagna this morning. I put it in the oven to heat and set the dial too high.

When we got home it was pretty charred. This is our first week in the house and I'm not familiar with the appliances."

He knew he sounded defensive. But he couldn't help it. Not considering the power this woman wielded. Her report could be a major factor in the court's decision about the future of the children.

"Moving can be very traumatic." Her tone was noncommittal. She refocused on Emily. "Do you like your new house?"

A vigorous nod preceded the little girl's response. "It's the bestest place Josh and I have ever lived."

"Maybe your uncle will give me a tour."

"Sure." Clay scanned the cluttered living room, trying to swallow past the lump in his throat. "We haven't finished unpacking yet. The extra boxes are all in here. The couch arrived yesterday, and I have a couple of chairs coming, too."

"You have no furniture of your own?" The woman was surveying the pile of dirty clothes in the middle of the floor.

"I was on my way to the washer when I heard Josh crying, and I dropped the clothes and ran." Clay answered her unspoken question first. "And no, I have very few possessions. I spent twelve years in the Army, and my job takes me all over the country. I didn't want to lug furniture with me from one place to another."

"Sounds like you're on the move a lot."

"In my current job I am. I'll be in Washington for another year, overseeing the construction of a large manufacturing plant. But I'm already looking for a position that will allow me to stay in one place."

He hadn't gotten very far with his search, however. For one simple reason. He couldn't decide where he wanted to live. The only place that had ever felt like home was Washington—for a lot of reasons he wasn't ready to consider. Yet this small town would never even have been on his radar screen, let alone his top-ten list, until a few weeks ago. He wasn't prepared to settle on it too fast.

The silence lengthened, and he realized the social worker was waiting for the rest of her tour. "Let me show you the kitchen," he offered, leading the way. The charred lasagna sat on the countertop, and a faint haze hung over the room. A card table and four chairs occupied the dinette area, and a stack of paper plates and plastic utensils sat in the middle.

"I have dishes and cutlery, but I haven't unpacked them yet," he told her.

The bathroom was in reasonable condition, as was his bedroom. Years of military training had taught him to keep his personal living quarters in tip-top shape. Most days, that philosophy carried over to the rest of the house. But his housekeeping had suffered during the past week, between the move and a few emergencies at work that had kept him laboring on paperwork long after Josh and Emily had gone to bed.

They moved on to the children's room, and Clay doubted she could find much fault there. He'd bought twin beds for them, and two matching dressers. Cate's mother had contributed a colorful mobile for the ceiling, and during the past week Cate had found bright, cheerful bedspreads and curtains. Anne had already taught Emily to make her bed in the morning, and she, in turn helped Josh. The room was in good shape.

"The children share a room?"

The woman's question deflated Clay's brief surge of optimism. He guessed that was a no-no.

"Yes." At this point, one-word answers were all he could manage.

By the time they completed their tour of the house and the

yard, and she spent a few minutes talking with the children, Clay wasn't merely discouraged—he was scared. And as he tried to quell his growing panic, he did something he hadn't done in years.

He prayed.

It wasn't an elaborate prayer. Just a few simple words. But his plea was heartfelt—and desperate.

Please, God. Give me one more chance.

Chapter Nine

"Cate? Clay. Did I catch you at a bad time?"

Though she tried to stifle the rush of pleasure at the sound of his mellow baritone on the other end of the phone, Cate didn't quite succeed. While she'd always considered her weekend break from child care duties essential to recharging her batteries, this job was different. Now the weekends dragged by. Thoughts of her young charges and their uncle—not always in that order—dominated her days, and her nights were filled with restless dreams that left her on edge when she awakened.

None of those were good signs, she knew. Not if she wanted to keep her distance from the apprentice father. But while she couldn't change her feelings, she didn't have to act on them. Polite, pleasant, helpful. That was the manner to strive for, she decided.

"No. I have a few minutes. What's up?"

"The social worker stopped by today. It was a disaster."

The bottom dropped out of her stomach. "What happened?"

Sliding onto a stool in her kitchen, she propped her elbow on the counter and listened with growing dismay as he gave her a recap. When he finished, she could only manage one word. "Wow."

"Yeah."

At his disheartened response, Cate's heart contracted in sympathy. *Lord, it isn't fair!* she protested in silence. *He's tried so hard. Please don't let him lose the kids because of this!*

"How are things now?"

"Quieter. I put the kids to bed early, and I'm not far behind. Pretty pathetic for a bachelor on a Saturday night, isn't it?"

"You've all had a trying day."

"We've had a trying three months. This was just the icing on the cake." He let out an exhausted breath. "Look, I'm sure you have better things to do than listen to my litany of woes. I promised myself I wouldn't bother you in your free time anymore, but I needed to hear a friendly voice. I'll let you get back to whatever you were doing."

She looked down at her left hand and tried to flex her fingers. Their sluggish response reminded her of one of the reasons she'd resolve to keep her distance from this man. Yet the words came out anyway.

"To be honest, I was thinking about you."

"Yeah?" There was a faint echo of hope in the word.

"Yeah." Then she forced herself to temper her response. "I was wondering if you remembered to replace the broken picket on the back fence. With Emily's fear of dogs, I'd hate for a stray to get into the yard while they were playing." That thought *had* crossed her mind a few minutes ago, so it wasn't a complete fabrication, Cate told herself.

"Oh." Disappointment edged out hope in his voice. "Yeah, I did it Friday night. Josh helped me. Meaning it took twice as long. But you know what?" Affection softened his tone. "I might have worked faster alone, but it wouldn't have been nearly as much fun. And I'm starting to think that might be true about a lot of things."

His subtle message wasn't lost on Cate. But she wasn't ready to have another discussion about them. Not yet. And maybe never.

"With the kids around, you won't have to worry about being alone for a very long time," she teased. "Now get some rest and I'll see you at church tomorrow."

She was grateful he didn't push. "Okay. Sorry again about disturbing you tonight."

As the line went dead, she slowly set the phone back in its cradle.

Disturbed was an apt way to describe her state of mind, Cate decided.

And it had nothing to do with an interrupted Saturday night.

"Clay! Could I speak with you for a minute?"

At Reverend Richards's call the next morning, Clay cast a longing glance at his truck. So much for his usual fast escape after Sunday services.

The minister hurried up to him and extended his hand. "I'm glad I caught up with you. However, you may not feel the same way after I tell you why," he added with a grin.

It was hard not to like the pastor. He was easygoing and down-to-earth, and he radiated empathy and caring. He also gave great sermons. The man's simple speaking style was compelling, his points always pertinent, and Clay was finding his message harder and harder to resist.

The God Reverend Richards spoke of bore little resemblance to the fierce, wrath-filled, vindictive figure he'd been taught to fear as a youth. As the pastor spoke in his unassuming style about the goodness of the Lord, His forgiving nature, His great love for the human race and His promise to be with us always, Clay began to experience a yearning to know Him better. To develop the kind of relationship with Him that seemed to provide comfort and guidance to the members of this small, close-knit congregation.

But the trust thing was hard to deal with. The letting go, the willingness to put yourself in God's hands, scared him. After his first seventeen years of living under his father's harsh rule, then another twelve dictated by the strict rules of military life, Clay had vowed to take control of his life. To make his own rules and live on his own terms. Turning his life over to God felt like a betrayal of the promise he'd made to himself. And he wasn't ready to do that.

The good news was that no one had pressured him to take that step. Including Cate. She knew he came to church only for the sake of the children. But while her faith was deep, and her devotion to the Lord solid and strong, she'd never tried to force her beliefs on him. She'd just gone about living her life according to the principles Reverend Richards spoke of each week. And in all honesty, that had done more to change his attitude toward religion than any words she could have said.

He was also grateful to Reverend Richards for respecting his decision to maintain a distance from the church. While the pastor had invited him and the children on numerous occasions to stay for the social hour after services, he always smiled and said, "Maybe another time," when Clay refused. There was no pressure, no handing out of guilt trips. That, too, appealed to Clay.

"What can I do for you, Reverend?" Clay returned the man's firm clasp.

"You may be sorry you asked that." The pastor gave a wry laugh. "But here's the gist of it. We're getting ready to build a picnic pavilion out back, where we can have socials and hold outdoor services in the nice weather. One of our members dabbles in architecture, and he put together a great design. But I'd feel better if someone with your background reviewed the plans, perhaps supervised the construction. We're going to have an old-fashioned one-day barn-raising to put it up. It will be a family event, with a picnic and activities for the children. I know how busy you are, but I'd be grateful if you could squeeze this in."

Clay frowned. Getting involved in a project like this wasn't going to help him keep his distance from the church community. On the other hand, he'd been coming to the services for more than two months, and other than putting some money in the collection basket, he'd done little to repay the warm welcome he'd received. It wouldn't kill him to review the plans and lend a hand for one day. And the kids would have fun. They needed to socialize more with children their own age, and this would be a good opportunity for that.

"Will Cate be there?"

Clay wasn't sure where that question had come from, but if Reverend Richards considered the query odd, he gave no indication.

"I'm sure she will. The whole Shepard clan will show up, I expect."

Weekend time with Cate. That clinched his decision. "Okay. I'll be happy to help."

"Great! If you can wait a few minutes, I'll dash over to the office and get the plans for you. Help yourself to some coffee and doughnuts downstairs if you like."

Clay wasn't ready to take that step yet. But he knew the kids would like him to accept the invitation. They'd asked him every Sunday if they could stay, and he'd always bribed them away with a promise of pancakes at a nearby diner. He steeled himself before looking down into the two sets of big eyes fixed on him.

"I like doughnuts." Josh's expression was hopeful.

"You can get a doughnut at the diner."

"Cate says they have the best doughnuts here," Emily added.

"Not today."

The kids let it drop, but their disappointment was obvious. And he felt like a heel. But he couldn't bring himself to make any more connections, to start any more relationships, to send down any more roots.

Suddenly he recalled what Pop had told the children about roots on moving day. How they helped stabilize you, protecting and strengthening you against storms. How they served as an anchor.

Clay could use some stability in his storm-tossed life about now, he reflected. And there were plenty of times he felt adrift.

Even so, he wasn't sure he was ready to drop anchor.

"Hi, Clay. It's Mark. I just checked my messages at the office and got yours from yesterday. Michelle and I are out of town for the holiday weekend. What's up?"

Shifting the phone on his ear, Clay stirred the spaghetti sauce he was heating for the kids' Sunday lunch. "The social worker showed up yesterday."

"I told you she'd be stopping by."

"Yeah, well, she couldn't have picked a worse time." Clay described her visit, sparing none of the gory details. When he finished, he braced himself for the worst. "What do you think?"

Mark's momentary silence was telling. "To be honest, I'd hoped she would walk away from her first visit with a better impression."

"What does this do to my chances?" Clay's tone reflected his mood. Flat and disheartened.

"Her report won't be based on one visit. She'll be back at least once more. Assuming things are more under control in the future, your chances should still be good. After all, everyone has an occasional bad day. I expect she'll take that into consideration. Try not to sweat this, Clay. It's over. Focus on doing everything you can to ensure she finds a less chaotic situation on her next visit."

"Yeah." Clay turned the stove off. "Listen, thanks for returning my call on a Sunday."

"No problem. I'll be in touch later this week."

As Mark hung up, Clay gave the spaghetti sauce one final stir, then crossed to the back door and pulled it open to scan the fenced yard. A few minutes ago the children had been playing on the swing. Now they were nowhere in sight.

A tingle of alarm raced down his spine, and Clay strode to the front of the house and opened the door. To his relief, the children were tossing a ball back and forth on the front lawn. But fear once more got the upper hand when Josh dashed toward the street to chase a wild throw by Emily—just as a car began to pass.

"Josh!" The urgency in his tone caught the boy's attention, and he stopped to turn toward his uncle. "Come up here!" Clay ordered, his voice raw. "You, too, Emily."

Mark's comment about the social worker replayed in Clay's mind as the children exchanged uncertain glances, then came slowly toward him.

Assuming things are more under control in the future, your chances should still be good.

Clay's blood ran cold as he imagined Ms. Douglas's reaction if she'd found the two children unsupervised and playing close to the street.

They stopped at the bottom of the two steps that led to the porch, anxiety etching their features. Clay planted his fists on his hips and glared at them, panic eating at his gut.

"I told you two to always stay in the backyard."

"It—it was muddy back there," Emily responded, subdued.

"That's no excuse. Josh almost ran in front of that car. He could have been killed if he'd gotten hit."

"I s-saw the car." Josh's lower lip started to quiver.

"You didn't act like you did," Clay snapped. "Emily, why didn't you try to stop him?"

"It happened too fast." Tears pooled in her eyes.

Josh edged closer to his sister, and she put a protective arm around his shoulders. "Please don't yell at E-Emily." A sob punctuated his plea. "Please don't be mad."

As Clay gazed down at them, huddled together several feet below him, he suddenly saw the situation from their perspective. They were at the mercy of an intimidating, angry man, just as they'd been at the mercy of the father they'd feared, who'd made them feel guilty for things that weren't their fault.

And today wasn't their fault, either.

They were only kids, Clay reminded himself. Trying to escape the mud, not being defiant. And Emily was only five. Though mature and conscientious beyond her years, she wasn't old enough to bear the burden of responsibility for her brother. Implying she was put inappropriate pressure on her.

If there had been any mistakes in the past few minutes, they'd been his, Clay realized. In his fear of losing the children, he'd overreacted to a situation that, while it needed to be addressed, didn't call for such severe treatment.

Taking a deep breath, Clay relaxed his posture and sat on the top step, putting himself on the same level as the children. From that vantage point, he had a clear view into their wide eyes, which reflected fear and insecurity—and that haunted look he'd first noticed in Nebraska.

Clay knew he had some bridges to mend. And a simple, "I'm sorry," wasn't going to cut it. Nevertheless, it was the place to start.

"Let's sit out here for a minute and talk, okay?" He gentled his tone and gestured to the concrete wall beside the steps that led to the porch, scooting over to give them room to pass.

The children complied, cutting a wide, wary berth around him. Once seated, Josh stuck his thumb in his mouth and Emily regarded her uncle in silence.

"First of all, I'm sorry I yelled. That was a wrong thing to do. But I was scared when I saw Josh run close to that car. I was afraid he'd get hurt. That's why we have the backyard rule. It's safer if you play there. And I want you to promise me you'll always stay inside the fence unless you're with me or Cate. Okay?"

"Okay." Emily dipped her head and scuffed the toe of her shoe against the concrete step. "Are you going to…to send us away?"

A shock wave reverberated through Clay at her whispered question. "Of course not. Why would you think that?"

"Sometimes, when Daddy got mad, he'd say he was going to send us to an orphan's home." Emily's voice quavered.

Clay gritted his teeth. Was there no end to the damage that monster had inflicted on his children? "That was a bad thing to say. When people make mistakes, you don't send them away. Or stop loving them."

"Do you love us?" Josh ventured.

Josh's wistful question startled Clay. He'd assumed the children were aware of his feelings. Why else would he be fighting to keep them? But he'd never put it into words. The admission implied too much. Love meant taking responsibility. Protecting. Sharing at the deepest levels. Opening yourself to risk.

Love was a loaded word.

Yet people needed to hear it, Clay acknowledged. Especially young children who had known far too little love in their lives, who had been taught by a bully of a father that love was contingent on behaving according to his standards. It was the same lesson Clay had learned from his own tyrannical father. The old man had never once told Clay he loved him, and he'd been clear that his love—and God's—was conditional, based on his son's ability to follow a set of rules so strict even Mother Teresa would have had trouble adhering to them.

It was time to break that pattern.

Moving slowly, he laid a hand on each of the children's shoulders. "I love you both very much." The words came out scratchy and rough, like the hinges on a door that hasn't been opened for a very long while. He cleared this throat and tried again. "You are the best thing that has ever come into my life."

Skepticism warred with hope in their eyes.

"Honest?" Josh said.

"Cross my heart," Clay told him.

"We've never been anybody's best thing." Wonder filled Emily's face. "Except Mommy's."

"We love you, too," Josh told him.

Swallowing past the lump in his throat, Clay smiled. "How about we go in and have some lunch?"

"Okay." Josh held out his arms, and Clay gave him a hug.

Emily leaned over and kissed his cheek. "We love you a whole bunch, too, Uncle Clay," she whispered.

The gentle, innocent love of the children touched him in a place that had long lain dormant, stirring up feelings that washed over him like a balmy tropical breeze.

And even though their spaghetti might be cold, his heart was warm.

Chapter Ten

"The social worker came by again this morning."

As Clay made the quiet comment, Cate stopped removing picnic items from the wicker hamper she'd packed for their fishing outing. The kids were down by the lake, getting a lesson on baiting hooks from Pop, giving them a minute alone. "How did it go?"

"Much better than the first visit. The kids were neat and clean, and chattering about today. The house was in good shape. I was cutting up vegetables in the kitchen to go with the dip."

She grinned. "Sounds even better than when she came last week while I was there."

Cate had given him a full report on the woman's second visit. She and the children had just finished baking cookies and Cate was telling them a story when the social worker had shown up. He'd assumed the woman had left with a good impression. Today's visit had gone equally well. That meant they had two good reports to counter the bad first visit two weeks ago.

"What happens next?" Cate asked.

"Mark says she may have enough material to write her report. After that, we wait for the hearing."

"I hate that things are unsettled." Frowning, she looked toward the children, who were talking in animated voices with Pop. Their giggles carried across the distance in the balmy, mid-June air. "I can't imagine putting them in an environment where there's no warmth or love or laughter. It would wipe out all the good we've been able to accomplish."

Clay agreed, though her use of the term *we* was generous, he acknowledged. While some of the credit for the children's great strides went to him, he knew the lion's share went to Cate. Without her, they'd be in an impersonal day care setting. Without her, his house would be a house—not a home filled with the smell of fresh-baked cookies and flowers from her garden and children's artwork adorning the refrigerator. Without her, he would long ago have crumbled under the awesome responsibility that had been thrust on him.

With each day that passed, it was becoming more and more difficult to imagine his life without her. Her gentle manner, kind heart, intuitive intelligence, courage, strength, sense of humor…they'd all enriched his life.

But what if he took the plunge—and failed? What if he chafed under the constraints that came with commitment? What if he couldn't give her the unfettered love she offered with such generosity to others—and which she deserved in return?

Yet when Cate turned toward him, her face awash with compassion and tenderness, his doubts dissolved. She always had that effect on him. In her presence, he felt like a ship that had been battered by storm-tossed seas but had at last found safe harbor. He felt as if he'd come home at last.

Somewhere in the recesses of his mind, a little voice reminded him of the hands-off promise he'd made to her a few weeks ago. He'd abided by it faithfully, tamping down the frequent impulse to seek opportunities to touch her. But today the urge was too strong to resist.

As their gazes locked, awareness zinging between them, he saw longing war with prudence in Cate's eyes. It was obvious she felt as strongly as he did—and just as obvious she was fighting it. Yet he could sense her restraint giving way, stretching like an overextended rubber band about to snap.

He took a step closer, never breaking eye contact. As he lifted his hand, a pulse began to beat an erratic rhythm in the delicate hollow of her throat. She swayed toward him, and he reached out to her…

"Uncle Clay! Uncle Clay! Look at this!"

Cate's eyes flew open, and as warmth tinted her cheeks a delicate pink, she moved away on the pretense of sorting through the picnic basket.

A powerful wave of disappointment swept over Clay as Josh skidded to a stop beside him clutching a small bird's nest. His fingers had been less than a heartbeat away from connecting with Cate's soft, satiny skin.

But perhaps he should be grateful for the interruption, Clay told himself. If he'd touched Cate, he would have broken his promise—and moved their relationship to a different level. And that wouldn't have been fair to her. He knew her reluctance to get involved stemmed, at least in part, from a concern that he wasn't ready for a house-with-a-white-picket-fence scenario. And for a woman from such a loving, stable family, that would be the only kind of relationship worth considering.

He understood her trepidation. And it was valid. While he might be willing to take responsibility for the children, putting a ring on a woman's finger…that required trust and sharing and communication and compromise. None of which he felt equipped to offer. Under Cate's tutelage, his fathering skills were improving. But that didn't mean he was husband material. Being a spouse required a whole different set of skills, and he didn't have a clue how to develop those.

It was better to keep following the plan they'd agreed upon weeks ago—let things rest for now.

Yet Clay couldn't help wishing Josh had waited just a little longer to claim his attention.

An hour later, after everyone had consumed their fill of Cate's fried chicken and potato salad, Clay took a sip of soda and exhaled a contented sigh.

Pop chuckled. "I'd take that as a compliment, if I were you," he told Cate, who'd risen to stow the remaining food in the cooler.

"Half the fun of a fishing trip is the picnic. Right, guys?" She winked at the two children as she set a bag of chocolate chip cookies on the table.

Josh helped himself to one. "I like picnics."

Grabbing a cookie, Emily swung her legs over the bench of the wooden picnic table. "Can we go down to the lake again?"

"Sure. But not by yourself." She looked at the two men.

"I'm too full to move," Pop declared.

"Me, too," Clay seconded. "We'll go back down a little later, Emily."

At their disappointed expressions, Cate caved. "Okay. I'll go with you guys. You two finish cleaning up." She tossed a roll of plastic wrap in Clay's direction.

He caught it with a grin. "Looks like I'm on KP."

"You had the opportunity for more pleasant duties," Cate replied pertly, taking the children's hands.

"Yeah. Missed opportunities seem to be my lot today." He held her gaze as he took a sip of soda.

Blushing, she turned away. "We'll be back in a little while."

Clay watched them, his grin softening into a tender smile. The three of them looked good together, he reflected. And right.

"Cate's sure got a way with kids," Pop commented.

"Yeah." Clay stretched his legs out in front of him. "I wish I had her knack."

"Don't sell yourself short. You're doing a fine job."

With a rueful shake of his head, Clay took another swig of soda. "Thanks, but I've made a lot of mistakes."

"That's what being a father is all about. Or a husband. You make mistakes, learn and try to do better the next time."

"Maybe. But I never expected to have to deal with family stuff."

"Not the marrying kind?"

"I never thought I was."

"It just takes the right woman to change a person's mind."

Clay sent an involuntary glance toward Cate. When he turned back, he wasn't sure he liked the gleam in Pop's eye. Doing his best to ignore it, he focused on selecting one of the cookies Cate had brought.

"At thirty, I'd sort of reconciled myself to being single, too, until my Mary Beth came along," Pop offered in the lengthening silence.

"What was it about her that changed your mind?" Clay finally chose a cookie.

"She was beautiful, for one thing. I always did have an eye for a pretty woman." He gave the younger man a wink. "But that wasn't why I fell in love with her. That happened more slowly, as I got to know her. She had a great capacity for love, plus tremendous courage and strength. I've always liked strong women. And I'd never met anyone stronger or braver than Mary Beth."

"How so?" Now Clay's interest was piqued.

Pop selected a cookie of his own. "It's a long story. Let me see if I can give you the short version." He took a bite and chewed for several seconds. "Mary Beth came from a single-parent household with five children, where love was doled out in meager portions. As the oldest, she was also expected to take on a lot of responsibility for the younger ones. She couldn't wait to get out, and six months before her high school graduation, she married a truck driver. Only it didn't have quite the happy ending she hoped for."

Chasing away a bee, Pop picked up his soda. "Things were okay until Mary Beth decided to get her GED. Her husband, who'd never finished high school, didn't much like that idea, but she did it anyway. After that, she started to talk about getting a degree. Took a second job to pay the tuition at the community college, and enrolled despite his disapproval. But he sabotaged her every step of the way. Even burned her books and a term paper, once."

"Are you serious?" Clay stared at him, appalled.

"Yes. And it got worse after she became pregnant with my stepson, Roger. I guess her husband figured that would slow her down, but instead she worked harder to give them a better life. That's when the physical abuse started. I'll spare you all the details, but it went on for several years. The neighbors called the police twice, and Mary Beth ended up in the emergency room more than once."

"Why didn't she leave him?" It was the same question Clay had asked himself over and over about Anne.

"In the end, she did."

"But why did she wait so long? The guy was a bum. She was better off without him."

"Just like your sister would have been?"

Pop's quiet question caught Clay off guard. "You know about Anne?"

"Only the basics. Cate's pretty close-mouthed about confidential client matters."

Clay wiped a hand down his face and set his uneaten cookie on the table. "I wanted her to leave years ago. But my father laid a guilt trip on her. Told her she'd fall from God's favor if she didn't honor her marriage vows." He didn't attempt to mask his bitterness.

"Guilt can be a powerful motivator," Pop conceded. "But there are all kinds of insidious ways to intimidate—or terrify—a woman into staying in an abusive relationship. Name-calling, put-downs, threats, forced isolation, withholding money. The list goes on and on."

Could some of those tactics have been factors in Anne's reluctance to leave Martin? Clay wondered. Was it possible the pressure his father had exerted from a religious perspective wasn't the only reason—or even the main reason—she'd stayed? It was a new and disturbing insight. One that merited more consideration, Clay decided.

"Anne had decided to leave her husband, too. The day before she died."

Pop laid a hand on his shoulder. "I'm sorry for your loss, son."

"At the funeral, the minister talked about how courageous she was." Clay swallowed hard. "I guess I never understood how true that was."

"Hold on to that thought, Clay." Pop squeezed his shoulder. "If she'd decided to leave, she had the same courage as my Mary Beth had. I'm just sorry her story didn't have the same happy ending."

* * *

Cate shaded her eyes and looked toward the picnic table. The two men were engrossed in what appeared to be a serious conversation. Good. After her almost-kiss with Clay, she needed a chance to regain her balance. And answering the children's eager questions about the lake and the fish, and how come stones skipped instead of sinking if you threw them at the correct angle, helped her do that.

"Is Pop really a grandfather?"

"Yes. He's my grandfather. And Rob's and Mark's." Cate lowered herself to the rock beside Emily. "Why?"

"He's not anything like our grandfather."

Cate had learned enough from Clay to know Emily's assessment was accurate. "Not all grandfathers are alike. And not all fathers are alike, either."

Emily pondered that. "Your daddy is nice."

"Yes, he is."

"Uncle Clay isn't a daddy, is he?"

"Well, he never had any children of his own. But sometimes a person can be a daddy without having their own children."

"How?"

"I had a friend once, whose mommy and daddy couldn't take care of her. When she was a little baby, they found a lady and a man who were married and who wanted a baby to love. So they gave that lady and man their baby to take care of forever. That's called adoption. And the lady and man became her new mommy and daddy."

"Was she happy?"

"Yes. Very happy."

"So…since my mommy is in heaven and my daddy is gone, could Uncle Clay adopt me and Josh?"

"He's figuring that out now with a judge. I know he wants you to stay with him, whether he adopts you or not."

"But if he adopted us, wouldn't that mean we'd never have to go live with our grandfather?" Emily persisted.

"Yes."

"Then I think he should adopt us. But…you know how you said your friend was adopted by a lady and man who were married?"

"Yes."

"Uncle Clay's not married."

"That's okay. He's your uncle. That makes a difference."

"But it would be okay if he *was* married, wouldn't it?"

"Yes."

"You're not married, are you, Cate?"

Suddenly Cate sensed where this was leading. "No, honey. I'm not."

"That means you could marry Uncle Clay, right?"

Cate stole a quick look at the man in question, who remained engrossed in conversation with Pop, and her heart did a little somersault.

Oh, yes! I could marry him—if I listened to my feelings instead of reason. And if my disabilities weren't a stumbling block.

"Cate?"

With an effort, Cate focused on Emily's question, trying to frame a noncommittal reply. "People only get married if they love each other, honey."

"Do you love Uncle Clay?"

She should have seen that coming, Cate berated herself.

"Look what I found!"

Josh thrust a frog in her face, and Cate recoiled with a squeal, leaving Emily's question unanswered.

But it continued to echo in her mind, reminding her that

even if she never gave Emily an answer, she needed to consider the question.

As well as the consequences.

Chapter Eleven

"Sorry to interrupt, Clay, but I have a Lieutenant Butler from the Omaha police department on line one for you. Shall I put him through?"

At Becky's question, Clay's grip tightened on the phone. "Give me a minute." He punched the hold button and turned to the electrical contractor. "Can we finish going over these revisions in a few minutes, Les? I need to take this call."

"Sure. I'll go keep Becky company. Let me know when you're ready." He shut the door to the construction trailer's small conference room as he exited.

"Okay, Becky." Clay waited as the connection went through. "This is Clay Adams."

"Mr. Adams, Lieutenant Butler in Omaha. I wanted to let you know we located Martin Montgomery."

Clay shut his eyes and expelled a long, relieved breath. But quick on the heels of relief came anger. And bitterness. "I hope you lock him up and throw away the key."

"Mr. Montgomery won't be using any taxpayer money. He

was killed in a barroom brawl in Oklahoma two days ago. We got a positive ID on the body a couple of hours ago."

As Clay absorbed the news, shock gave way to resentment. He'd wanted retribution. Wanted to see the man caught and punished. Wanted to see him suffer as he'd made Anne suffer.

On the other hand, Martin's violent end gave Clay a sense of vindication. Someone had bullied the abuser, hurt him, as he'd hurt Anne. It seemed fitting, somehow.

From everything he'd learned since attending the church in Washington, Clay knew he shouldn't feel this way. That he should somehow dredge up compassion for the man, even forgive him. But he couldn't. Not after what he'd done to Anne. And to his children. The man was scum. He'd deserved the end he'd met.

Though his emotions were churning, his response was calm. "Thank you for letting me know, Lieutenant."

"I know this doesn't bring your sister back, Mr. Adams. But I hope it will give you some sense of closure."

As Clay hung up, he realized the news did provide an end to one part of the story. Anne's husband could never hurt anyone again. His death was no great loss, and Clay doubted anyone would miss the man. Least of all his children.

But they still had to be told. And he didn't relish the job. While he could see definite signs of healing, they remained as fragile as a butterfly's wing. They were too attuned to nuances, and a brusque tone, aggravated glance or irritated gesture could devastate them. Insecurity remained a problem, too. They craved approval and were hyper-sensitive to criticism.

Clay had no idea how they would react to this news. But he did know it needed to be handled with the proverbial kid gloves. Not the kind he'd ever had much occasion to wear until Josh and

Emily entered his life. And if he blew this, in one fell swoop he could wipe out all the progress the kids had made.

He needed help.

He needed Cate.

As he reached for the phone to call her, it occurred to him that a request for help from the Lord might not be out of order, either.

His hand stilled as he thought back to some of the bible stories Reverend Richards had talked about over the past few weeks. The loaves and the fishes. The wedding at Cana. The storm on the lake. The death of Lazarus. All tales of people turning to the Lord for help. And He hadn't failed any of them.

Yet the concept of prayer remained foreign to Clay. Even in church, he felt awkward about it. But no one would know about this prayer, except the Lord. If He was listening. And if He was, if He was as loving and benevolent and caring as the people in Reverend Richards's congregation believed, surely He would overlook an error in form, or a few stumbles.

Closing his eyes, he spoke in the silence of his heart.

Lord, You know I haven't been Your most faithful servant. For years I turned my back on You because I thought You were vindictive and revengeful. But I'm beginning to think I may have been wrong. That the information I was given as a child was ill-informed and misinterpreted. If You're the compassionate God Reverend Richards talks of, please help me handle this well with the children.

As Clay finished, an odd sense of peace enveloped him. It wasn't as if all his problems had been solved. Far from it. But for the first time, he felt that perhaps some greater power was on his side.

And since he needed all the reinforcements he could get, he dialed the number that would connect him with the woman who had been on his side from the start.

* * *

Two hours later, Cate heard the slam of the truck door as she cleaned up the last of the craft supplies from the kitchen table. She and Clay had talked strategy on the phone, and they'd decided he should finish out his workday. Any change in routine made the children anxious, and an early homecoming would raise their suspicions. Cate and Clay had agreed it was important for the children to feel relaxed and secure when they heard the news.

Cate had promised to read them a story before she left, but she'd managed to distract them with the special craft project they were stashing now in their room. Retrieving the book from the top of the refrigerator, she laid it on the table as Clay opened the back door. The kids had memories like elephants, and she was counting on them holding her to her word about the story.

As Clay stepped across the threshold, that all-too-familiar flutter quivered in Cate's stomach. She'd never met a man with such intense magnetism. And nothing detracted from it. Not the smudge of exhaustion under his eyes. Not the mud-splattered jeans or grimy cotton shirt rolled to the elbows that revealed tanned forearms. Not the tense line of his jaw.

If anything, she had to fight the temptation to reach up and tenderly smooth away the deep grooves of worry and weariness carved beside his mouth and between his eyes.

That not being an option, she needed to find some other way to loosen him up. His tension was almost palpable, and the children would pick up on it in a heartbeat, foiling their plan.

Locking her hands behind her back to keep them out of trouble, she put the kitchen table between them and tried for a teasing tone. "The kids will be back any second. I'll give you a chocolate chip cookie if you smile."

For a moment his face went blank. Then, as he got her message, he rolled his head and flexed his shoulders. "Better?"

She tipped her head and studied him. "A little. How about if I raise the ante to two cookies?"

"That's a good incentive." He seemed to relax a bit more.

"It always works with Josh and Emily."

"I can think of a more grown-up treat that would be far more effective." He smiled, cast a lingering look at her lips, and waggled his eyebrows.

His sassy response did nothing to steady her pulse, but at least he was more relaxed now.

"Hi, Uncle Clay." Josh zoomed through the door and launched himself into Clay's arms.

Emily was close on his heels, grabbing the storybook on the table as she passed.

After hugs were exchanged, Emily waved the book at Cate. "You promised you'd read this to us before you left."

"You're right. I did." Cate gestured toward the living room. "Let's cuddle up on the couch. Maybe Uncle Clay will come, too."

As two expectant little faces tipped up toward him, Clay called up a smile. "I could use a good story."

He followed them into the living room, where the two children settled beside Cate on the couch. Wedging himself into one corner, he angled his body to observe the domestic scene playing out beside him.

Clay paid little attention to the fairy tale. He was more focused on the slender, blond-haired woman who was reading the words in a lilting, animated voice that kept the children enthralled. And it was easy to see why. She gave them her absolute attention, reaching out to stroke Emily's hair or give Josh's hand a squeeze as she read, demonstrating her instinctive ability to discern—and provide—what people needed. And if her kindness and unselfish generosity had endeared her to the children, it had done no less with him. If he wasn't careful, he'd begin to think in terms of the L word.

And maybe that wasn't such a bad thing, Clay acknowledged.

He'd dodged commitments for more than twenty years. And it had been an effective strategy for keeping his heart safe. His existence might have been emotionless, but he hadn't inflicted damage on anyone, nor had anyone hurt him.

Yet now that he was surrounded by caring people, he recognized that while his previous life might have been safe, it had also been lonely.

Very lonely.

"…And they lived happily ever after."

"I like happily-ever-afters," Emily declared. "Does happily-ever-after really happen, or is it only in stories?"

"What do you think?" Cate asked, closing the book.

"I guess it can happen. Like that friend of yours who was 'dopted when she was a little girl." Emily's expression grew wistful. "Are we going to have a happily-ever-after?"

Cate looked at Clay. This was the handoff they'd discussed. She'd set the stage. The kids were as happy, relaxed and receptive as they'd ever be. He was on.

"I'm going to do everything I can to make sure you do." At Clay's comment, both children's heads swiveled toward him. "You know what? My lap feels awfully empty."

Josh scooted off the couch at once, scrambling past Emily to climb up Clay's knee. He settled the boy against his chest and tugged Emily closer, tucking her beside him. Cate perched on the arm of the couch, her support and encouragement the only thing keeping him afloat as he entered these treacherous waters.

Summoning up his courage, he plunged in. "I had some news

today about your daddy." The children stiffened, and there was an immediate change in the rhythm of their breathing.

"He's not coming back for us, is he?" Emily looked up at him with wide, frightened eyes.

"No, honey. He's never coming back. A policeman from Omaha called to tell me your daddy was in a fight. He got hurt, and he…he died."

He watched their faces as they struggled with that concept.

"You mean…like Mommy?" Emily's forehead puckered.

"Yes."

"He can't hurt Mommy in heaven, can he?" Josh asked in alarm.

Clay doubted the man was anywhere close to heaven. Not if there was any justice. But he framed his reply with care. "He can never hurt your mommy again."

"That's good." Relief smoothed the tension from Josh's features. "He wasn't very nice. He made Mommy cry."

"I'm glad he's gone." Emily's tone was defiant, her eyes fierce. "He was mean. I like it much better here with you, Uncle Clay."

"Me, too," Josh seconded.

His fears had been groundless, Clay realized, as his tense muscles went limp. The children's only concern had been for their mother, and their father's ability to hurt her beyond the grave. There was no sense of loss. Which was fine with Clay. As far as he was concerned, the man didn't deserve one second's worth of mourning.

"I like it better with you here, too. It was much too quiet before." He tickled Josh's tummy, eliciting a giggle.

"Can we eat dinner now? I'm hungry," Emily declared.

"Sure. Why don't you guys set the table while I say goodbye to Cate."

After hugs were dispensed and Cate retrieved her purse, Clay followed her to the front door.

"I can't believe how smoothly that went." Clay took a deep breath. "The only emotion I picked up was relief."

"With good reason, from what I've gleaned about their father. He was nothing more to them than a threat. You handled it well, by the way."

"I wouldn't have, without you."

She made a dismissive gesture. "You did all the hard work. I just read a story."

"You were here. That made all the difference." He propped a shoulder against the door frame and shoved one hand in the pocket of his slacks. He was stepping onto shaky ground, but he didn't care. In addition to being grateful for her support, he found her incredibly appealing in the soft, pink knit top that emphasized her curves and khaki shorts that revealed her long, lovely legs. "I don't suppose I could convince you to stay for dinner, could I?"

Caution flared in her eyes even before she folded her arms across her chest and took a step back. "I told Michelle I'd go shopping with her tonight for baby furniture."

Drop it, he told himself. She's already skittish. Yet the question came out anyway. "Is that the only reason?"

She gave him a wary look. "I thought we were going to table a discussion of personal matters for a while."

"I'm starting to regret that agreement."

"I'm not." She edged the screen door open. "Let's leave things as they are for now. Be sure to sprinkle some parmesan cheese on the casserole when you take it out of the oven. The kids like that."

And then she was gone.

He stayed in the doorway as she slid into her car. Watched her back out of his driveway. Waited until her car disappeared around the corner.

She never looked back.

As he closed the door and flipped the lock, Clay mulled over his next steps. And ran through a list of questions that were beginning to demand answers.

Was he ready to make the kind of commitment a woman like Cate would expect?

Was it fair to her to act on the attraction between them if he wasn't?

Should he see how things went with the family responsibilities he'd accepted before taking on any more?

Why was Cate so skittish?

What impediments did she see to a relationship?

Were they surmountable?

Clay didn't have any of those answers. But before too much more time passed, he'd have to seek them out.

Because he knew they held the key to his future.

As the children knelt at their beds later that evening—a ritual Anne had taught them, and one they continued to follow—Clay rested an arm on the dresser. He was used to the routine by now. They always said the same prayer, in unison, then asked God to take care of certain people at the end, each contributing names.

The list was pretty familiar to Clay, though it kept growing. Anne was always first, followed by him and Cate. Pop had been added weeks ago. Other members of Cate's family came next. Reverend Richards had joined the list at some point, along with assorted people they'd come to know as they did errands each day with Cate. The lady at the bakery who always gave them a cookie. The librarian who set aside special books for them. The waitress at the diner on Sunday who always managed to bring them a special treat "on the house."

As they finished, Emily gave Clay an uncertain look. "Should we pray for Daddy, too?"

His first inclination was to say no. The man didn't deserve their prayers. But there was no question he needed them. And Clay knew what Reverend Richards would say, if asked the same question. Or Cate.

"Yes, honey, I think that's a good idea."

"How about Grandpa?"

That was harder. Praying for a man who could never inflict any more harm was one thing. It was a magnanimous gesture. Sanctioning prayers for someone who remained a threat, who had the potential to ruin the lives of these children, was harder. And Clay wasn't inclined to be that generous. But perhaps his old man needed the prayers most of all, Clay conceded. His stay on earth wasn't over yet. A chance remained—however slim—that, with the grace of God, he would see the light and mend his ways.

"It couldn't hurt," he told her.

The children concluded, mentioning their grandfather last. While Clay didn't hold out a lot of hope their prayer would have much impact, it was possible God would listen to these little children and work a miracle.

Because nothing less would soften his father's heart.

"What's this?" Clay picked up the envelope on the kitchen table. His name had been printed in crude lettering on the front with a green crayon—by Emily, he assumed. With lots of coaching from Cate.

The two children beamed up at him. "Happy Father's Day!"

Clay's hand froze, and his heart did a funny somersault. He'd forgotten it was Father's Day. The day had never meant anything to him, as a child or as an adult. And since he'd never planned on having a family, he'd never expected to get a Father's Day card. Receiving one gave him an odd feeling in his chest. Not bad, but…different. Warm. And full. And good.

Stunned, Clay sat at the table. The children pressed close on each side, watching in excitement as he lifted the flap and withdrew the card that proclaimed him as a "special uncle."

"Cate helped us pick it out," Josh told him. "But we each signed our name."

With hands that weren't quite steady, he opened it, read the sentiment, and looked at the sprawling printed names at the bottom and on the inside of the cover. Emily had added a flower and a smiling face above her name, and Josh's drawing resembled a fishing pole and a swing. Sort of.

"Do you like it?" Emily's eyes were anxious.

"It's the best present I ever got." Clay choked out the words.

"But we have presents, too!" Josh declared. He scampered into their bedroom, returning a minute later with two small boxes. "This one's from me." He thrust a gaily wrapped package at Clay.

His fingers fumbling, Clay pulled off the paper and withdrew a small wooden picture frame. Stones and acorn shells and twigs had been glued around the edges, and inside the frame was a photo of Josh and Emily holding fishing poles, their faces split by huge grins.

"I glued the stuff on the frame," Josh said. "Cate helped me collect it. And she took the picture. Do you like it?"

There was an apprehensive note in his question, and Clay gave him a tender smile. "It's wonderful, Josh. I'm going to take this to work and put it on my desk. That way I can see you and Emily even when I'm not with you."

Josh beamed as Emily held out her package. Inside Clay discovered a shallow box, open on the top, constructed of popsicle sticks. It was painted bright blue and decorated with buttons.

He had no idea what it was.

"Cate says you can use it for stuff on your desk at work," Emily offered.

Grateful for the clue, he smiled. "It's perfect."

And it was. Both gifts were. Maybe the edges didn't quite line up on the desktop caddy. Maybe the decorations on the frame weren't quite straight. But the love represented by the gifts was perfect. And it meant the world to him.

He told that to Cate later, pulling her aside after the worship service while Pop kept the children occupied. She shook her head, however, at his thanks.

"I wish I could take the credit. But Emily came up with the idea." She smiled at him, her eyes soft green pools in the dappled shade of morning as she rested her hand on his arm. "They love you a lot, Clay. And that kind of love can't be bought or bribed or bartered. Especially from children. You've done a great job."

The children's gifts had filled him so full of happiness Clay hadn't thought there was room for any more. But Cate's words of praise were the icing on the cake. A torrent of emotion overwhelmed him, and he suddenly found it difficult to breathe.

She turned away before he could speak, taking the warmth of her hand from his arm.

But in its place, she left a warm glow in his heart.

Chapter Twelve

Clay lifted his elbow and wiped his forehead on the sleeve of his T-shirt, then took a long, cold swig of lemonade. In typical Missouri fashion, the late June Saturday afternoon was hot, muggy and uncomfortable. But the heat hadn't deterred the dozens of congregants who'd shown up at church to lend a hand with the pavilion-raising project.

From his vantage point across the property, Clay examined the results of their labors. The structure of the cedar pavilion was in place, and the willing, if unskilled, crew was diligently working on the floor and railings. Children played in a safe area off to one side, and an abundance of home-cooked food was being set out for a late lunch in the shade of a towering oak tree.

Reverend Richards, dressed in blue jeans and a T-shirt, broke apart from the cluster of people wielding hammers and saws and headed toward Clay. "I'm glad to see you're taking a much-needed break."

"To be honest, I feel a little guilty about it. Everyone else is still hard at it."

"They're a good group." The minister surveyed the scene. "I

was very blessed to receive a call from this church when I was ordained four years ago."

"You mean you weren't always a preacher?" Clay had assumed the man had spent all of his adult life in ministry.

"Far from it. I worked for quite a few years in the corporate world first."

Intrigued, Clay cocked his head. "What did you do?"

"I was vice president of planning for a pretty sizable company."

When he named a firm on the Fortune 500 list, Clay's eyebrows rose. Bob Richards had been a successful business executive, with all the perks and prestige that came with a coveted position in a blue-chip firm. And he'd walked away to be a small-town pastor.

It didn't compute.

"Wasn't that a lot to give up?"

The minister smiled. "I found something better."

His response surprised Clay. What was it about being a minister that had been compelling enough to induce him to make such a radical change in lifestyle?

"Had you always been drawn to the ministry?" Clay ventured.

The pastor gave a rueful laugh. "No. In my younger days I barely had a speaking acquaintance with the Lord. My sights were set on a business career, and the Lord didn't fit in with my plans. I wanted to be rich and powerful, and in the eyes of the world I achieved that."

"So what happened?"

"No bolt from the blue, if that's what you mean. I just began to realize that despite the money and the power and the perks, I wasn't happy. Nor did I feel grounded or secure. I knew some essential component was missing from my life, but I couldn't quite figure out what it was. I only knew I felt restless."

The minister stuck his hands in his pockets, his expression reflective. "Over time, though, I began to hear a voice. *His* voice. Calling me home. Only I didn't want to go. It was way too scary. And the sacrifices required were too great. He was asking me to give up everything I'd worked for, change the plan for my life. And I didn't want to do that. I liked being in charge of my destiny, and I was afraid to relinquish that control. I fought Him every step of the way."

"What happened to change your mind?"

Reverend Richards refocused on Clay. "The voice kept growing stronger, always gentle, but always there. Until I conceded that I needed to at least consider what He was asking. And once I opened that door, once I allowed for the possibility that maybe God had a different idea about what He wanted for my life than I did, the rest fell into place. I left my job, went to divinity school, and now I'm content serving the Lord in this small church in Washington, Missouri."

The man's story resonated with Clay, touching on many of the emotions he'd been experiencing in the past few months. The restlessness. The feeling that some essential element was missing. The fear of letting go, of relinquishing control. Even the need to connect with the Lord and understand His will.

Except Reverend Richards had found his answers. Clay's search continued.

"I envy you your sense of contentment," Clay admitted.

"It didn't happen overnight. But in the end, my life played out the way it was supposed to. If I'd come to ministry sooner, I wouldn't have brought with me as many insights about the pressures and temptations of the business world or understood the struggle to hear God's voice."

The pastor shifted his position to take advantage of the protective shade of a sheltering maple tree. "You know, I used to envy those whose beliefs have been solid and sure since childhood. But those of us who struggle to understand and accept bring a special gift to the faith. And it's encouraging to know the history of Christianity is full of holy people who grappled with doubt and temptation. They serve as a great reminder that God calls us by many different paths to His truths, and that He calls us *all*—sinners and saints alike. We just have to listen for His call and say 'yes' when the time comes."

Clay swirled the ice in his lemonade, watching it melt in the warmth of the sun. "I think I fall more into the sinners category. I haven't had much of a relationship with the Lord. To be honest, I wouldn't be at church now if it wasn't for the children."

"The Lord often works in interesting ways, doesn't He?" The minister's lips tipped up into a gentle smile. "And as for being a sinner, we all are, Clay. We're human. God doesn't expect us to be perfect. He just expects us to try."

"I don't think I'm ready to take the leap of faith you did," Clay confessed. "But I've begun to recognize there's a hole in my life. And I'm beginning to think part of what's missing is a relationship with the Lord."

"Then you've taken the first step. The rest will come, if you listen for His voice and open your heart." He gestured toward the tables of food, where a hungry horde had gathered. "Now let's go have some lunch. And a word to the wise: Be sure to try the apple cobbler in the big white casserole. That's my wife's contribution, and if you'll pardon me for bragging, she makes the best cobbler in Franklin County."

"Say, Pop, what's the story on that guy?" Clay snagged a can of soda from an oversized cooler and flipped the top.

Pop followed the direction of Clay's gaze toward Dan Maxwell, who was hammering a floorboard into the pavilion. His eyes narrowed. "What do you mean?"

"You have an odd expression. The same one you had when he stopped to talk to Cate a few weeks ago after services. Like you don't like him."

"Hmph. So much for my acting ability. And Christian charity. I'll have to work on both."

"Cate had an odd expression that day, too."

After a brief hesitation, Pop took Clay's arm and drew him away from the work crew putting the finishing touches on the pavilion. "I'm not one for gossip, but I guess it's time you knew about Cate and Dan."

He turned his back toward the tall, blond man with the athletic build and vivid blue eyes. "Dan came to Washington about five years ago and joined our congregation. I suppose he's the kind of man who can turn a woman's head. Handsome, in a Nordic kind of way. Excellent manners. Churchgoing. He and Cate started dating, and things got pretty serious. We all expected an engagement announcement any day. Then, out of the blue, it was over."

"What happened?"

"I don't know." Pop scratched his head. "Cate never talked much about it. All she said was that things didn't work out and they weren't going to be seeing each other anymore. There was no acrimony between them. But Cate changed after that. Got quieter, and resigned. Whatever Dan did killed her dreams of finding a man to love, of having a family."

Clay scrutinized the blond-haired man. His wife had joined him now, bouncing their baby on her shoulder. Dan tousled the little one's head and leaned over to kiss his wife's forehead. They were the picture of a loving family.

"For the record, I don't much care for people who hurt the ones I love."

Picking up the warning in the older man's tone, Clay leveled a steady look in his direction. "I feel the same way."

Pop perused him in silence, then gave a slow nod. "That's good to know." He folded his arms across his chest. "Cate hitched a ride with me this morning. But Joe, my buddy from the garden club, asked me to take in a movie tonight. I'd sure like to go."

"I could give her a lift home."

"I was hoping you could." There was a twinkle in the older man's eyes.

He started to walk away, but Clay put a hand his arm. "Thanks, Pop."

A smile touched the corners of the older man's lips. "Sometimes you just have to trust your heart."

As Pop strolled away, Clay downed the rest of his soda and regarded Dan Maxwell again. He understood Pop's feelings about Cate's one-time suitor. He shared them. Cate didn't deserve to be hurt, and he didn't have much respect or tolerance for anyone who had caused her pain.

Yet might he be setting himself up to do the same? he wondered. He hadn't made any secret about his attraction to her, and he was pretty sure it was mutual. But what if things heated up and he got scared? He could end up jilting her, as Dan had. And that wasn't good. The last thing he wanted to do was hurt the lovely woman who had added such joy to his life.

Scanning the women setting out the food for the potluck supper, Clay had no trouble spotting Cate, with her mane of blond hair. She was cutting a layer cake at the dessert table.

Suddenly she glanced up, as if she'd sensed his scrutiny across the lawn, and her hand stilled. She was too far away for him to read her eyes, but he didn't imagine the jolt of electricity that arced between them.

A soft blush turned her peaches-and-cream complexion pink, and she froze. A few charged seconds ticked by, and then she tucked her hair behind her ear and went back to work.

Crushing the empty aluminum can in his hand, Clay drew a long, steadying breath. His instincts told him to ignore the warning signs flashing in his mind. But his innate sense of honor wouldn't let him. He couldn't act on his feelings unless he came to grips with his commitment phobia and put to rest the fear that he wasn't husband material.

But how was he supposed to do that?

Pray.

The single word echoed in his mind—perhaps triggered by his conversation with Pastor Bob, he theorized. But it wasn't a bad idea. And he didn't have any better ones.

Turning away from the crowd converging on the food tables, Clay tipped his head back and focused on the blue expanse of sky.

Lord, please guide me. I don't want to hurt Cate. But I'm beginning to believe she and I were meant to be together. Help me overcome my fears and give me the courage to follow my heart, trusting You to steady me if I falter. And please help Cate deal with whatever is holding her back, too. Because I sense her obstacles are as potent as my fears.

Cate felt as if she'd just run a marathon.

Shifting away from the group of women setting out casseroles on the long table next to hers, she began to divvy up the slices of cake among paper plates as she struggled to catch her breath.

No longer could she dodge the truth. Not after those amazing few seconds, when one look at Clay had short-circuited her vital signs.

She had to face the facts.

Despite her vow to keep her distance, the handsome engineer who'd come to town to build a manufacturing plant had also managed to build a bridge between their hearts.

And that was dangerous.

Or was it?

For the first time, Cate allowed for the possibility that maybe her heart didn't need protecting. From Clay, anyway. Over the past few months, as she'd watched this man who'd claimed to be rootless, anti-religion and commitment-averse move to a house, connect with a church and take responsibility for two traumatized children, putting their needs above his own, he'd shaken her resolve to steer clear of romance. From everything she could see, Clay Adams was a good, decent man well worth the risk of loving.

But she'd thought the same about Dan.

And paid the consequences.

"Everything okay, Cate?"

Her hand jerked, and a piece of cake plopped icing-side-down on the Formica-topped table.

"Hi, Marge." She shot the picnic chairwoman an apologetic glance. "Yes, I'm fine. Sorry about this." It took her two attempts to scoop up the cake. Not because one of her hands had limited use, but because both were trembling. A fact the gray-haired woman had no doubt noticed, Cate concluded in dismay.

"No problem. We have cake coming out our ears. You sure you're okay? The heat's not getting to you, is it?" The woman fanned herself with her hand and shook her head. "Could Pastor Bob have picked a hotter day?"

Disposing of the cake in a nearby trash can, Cate wiped her hands on a napkin and latched onto Marge's explanation. "It's pretty intense for the end of June. I think I'll grab a cup of lemonade."

"Good idea. Then get a plate of food for yourself before it's all gone. We've got one hungry crew here."

The woman moved away, and Cate gave the table one more swipe to erase any lingering evidence of her faux pas. Risking a peek across the lawn, she noted that Clay remained apart from the group, his back to her. He was looking up, his posture contemplative.

As if he was praying.

Was that possible? she wondered. While his attitude toward religion had softened, she didn't think he'd yet put the power of prayer to work in his life.

But whether he had or not, it was time she did, Cate resolved.

Because the decisions she faced in the coming weeks were too big for her to handle alone.

"Sorry Pop cornered you about giving me a lift. I could have hitched a ride with someone else in my family." Cate retrieved her purse from the floor of Clay's truck as he pulled into a parking space in front of her condo.

"I didn't mind the detour." He set the brake and checked out Josh and Emily over his shoulder. They were sound asleep in their car seats, and his mouth softened into a smile. "Looks like I won't be missed if I walk you to your door."

Cate shifted around to observe the youngsters in the deepening twilight. "Josh missed his nap, and Emily was wired all day. But they had a blast playing with all the other kids. They'll sleep well tonight."

"So will their uncle." Clay grinned and unbuckled his seat belt. "Sit tight."

Half a minute later, he pulled open her door and she swiveled in the seat. Rather than let her struggle out of the high cab, he reached up and circled her slender waist with his hands. As he swung her to the ground, she instinctively grasped his shoulders.

She felt good in his arms, he reflected, as he stared down into her wide, clear eyes. Soft and feminine and oh-so-appealing. He wouldn't mind standing like this for the rest of the night.

Or the rest of his life, he realized.

Only when she gently attempted to pull away did he release her.

"You can say goodbye here, Clay." There was a hint of panic in her voice. "Take the kids home and get some rest."

"I'll rest better if I'm sure you're safe inside."

He thought she was going to object, but in the end, with a shrug of capitulation, she acquiesced. Taking her arm, he fell into step beside her, shortening his stride to match hers.

"Sorry. I'm a bit slow tonight." Her apology came out breathless.

"I'm in no hurry."

In the four months he'd known Cate, he could never remember her being this nervous. He could feel the apprehension radiating from her as they approached her door. Heard her keys rattling in her hand as she withdrew them from her purse. Saw the quiver in her fingers as she tried twice to slip her key into the lock before succeeding. It was obvious the moment on the church lawn was etched in her memory, as it was in his.

"Hey. It's okay." His words came out in a husky whisper as he stroked her arm below the sleeve of her soft knit shirt.

Slowly she lifted her head from the lock to focus on his fingers against her skin. "It doesn't feel okay."

"You don't like this?" He continued to stroke her arm.

"What h-happened to our hands-off agreement?"

She'd avoided his question, he noted. Meaning she liked his touch. But she was scared.

Forcing himself to break contact, he shoved his hands into his pockets. "I think we should revisit it."

When she at last lifted her chin and allowed him to look into her eyes, he saw conflict, fear and yearning. It was impossible to tell which was stronger. But the pulse fluttering in the hollow of her throat and her soft, parted lips called out to him.

Earlier, he'd prayed for the courage to follow his heart. So without agonizing further, he leaned down and touched his lips to hers.

He half expected her to pull away. But she didn't move. Instead, much to his surprise, she kissed him back. Thoroughly.

Clay stretched the kiss out as long as he dared, resisting the temptation to let it escalate. Finally, calling on every ounce of his willpower, he drew back long before he was ready to release her.

For several seconds, her eyes remained closed, the long sweep of her lashes resting on her fair skin. When at last they fluttered open, her pupils were a bit dilated. She swallowed. Blinked. Took a deep breath.

"That wasn't fair." Her whispered comment was ragged.

"I followed the rules." He leaned back a little and wiggled his fingers, still in his pockets. "Hands off."

"In letter only."

He conceded the point with a shrug. "Are you sorry?"

"I don't know." She folded her arms across her chest and eased away, a frown marring her smooth brow. "Pursuing this could be a mistake. For both of us."

"Why?"

She shook her head and fumbled for the handle of the door behind her. "It's too complicated to go into tonight."

"We need to talk about this, Cate. I know there are issues. Our backgrounds are different. And when we met, our approach to life was different, too. But a lot of things have changed over the past few months."

"This isn't the time for that discussion. I'm going to hold you to your promise about tabling it until after the custody issue is resolved. I need some space to think things through."

Clay wanted to press, but his instincts told him to back off. Weeks ago, Cate had said she wasn't willing to risk testing their compatibility. It was clear she still considered him a risky proposition. And she might be right, he admitted. Before he dived into romance, he needed to be absolutely sure about his intentions. While he was close to accepting the notion of commitment, he wasn't there yet.

And it was clear the woman across from him suspected that.

"Okay." He stepped back. "We'll do this your way. Goodnight, Cate."

Returning to his truck, he climbed into the driver's seat and checked on the kids. Still snoozing, he noted, one corner of his mouth twitching. No surprise there. As Cate had pointed out, after their exhausting day they'd no doubt sleep like logs all night.

He was tired, too. But he had a strong suspicion his two little charges would greet the morning a whole lot more rested than he would.

Chapter Thirteen

"We have a court date, Clay. August fourth in Omaha."

At Mark's news, Clay flipped to the next page in his calendar, juggling the phone as he jotted a note on the day the court would decide whether he could keep Josh and Emily. A month away. His gut clenched and he leaned forward in his desk chair, every muscle tense. "Is there anything else we can do while we wait?"

"I've checked all the references you provided. Your military record is outstanding, and your boss speaks well of you. I also talked with Reverend Richards, as you suggested. His endorsement will have a lot of impact. The only loose end is the job situation. Have you had any luck finding a position that requires less travel? The judge will ask about that."

"Yeah. I talked to my boss. Our work in the St. Louis area is increasing, and they're thinking of opening a branch in the city. He said the area supervisor position is mine if the expansion goes through, but that won't be decided for several months. If it doesn't happen, I'll find a more stable job."

"Let's hope that satisfies the judge. Also, I just got a copy of the report from the social worker. You passed with flying colors."

Clay let out a long breath. "That's the best news I've had in weeks."

"I think we have a good case, Clay. Try not to lose sleep over this."

As he hung up, Clay wished he could follow Mark's advice. But until he had official papers in his hand saying Josh and Emily belonged with him, he knew he wouldn't rest easy.

"Hey, Clay, thanks again for helping with the pavilion. We couldn't have done it without you."

Clay looked up from his seat on a blanket on the church grounds, searching his memory for the name of the man who'd worked on the building crew the prior weekend. "I was glad to help, Ralph. But you people did all the real work."

The man chuckled. "My father wasn't much of a handyman, but he swung a mean hammer. At least I learned how to pound a nail in straight." He inspected the pavilion, where Reverend Richards had conducted a special Fourth of July service in conjunction with the dedication of the structure. "Turned out real fine. Well, enjoy your picnic."

As the man headed back to his family, Clay scanned the church grounds. Members of the congregation had brought picnic dinners to enjoy after the service and dedication, and several had stopped to thank Clay for his help with the project. That sense of belonging was a new experience for him, one he'd always taken great pains to avoid. But it didn't feel at all confining or uncomfortable, as he'd expected. On the contrary. It felt good.

"I like this." Emily held up her fork to examine the spiral noodle she'd speared. "What is it?"

"Pasta salad," Cate told her, directing a smile toward Clay. "And I second that. The food is great."

"I can't claim any credit for it. I threw myself on the mercy of a nice older woman at the deli on Main Street. She put the menu together." He hadn't been sure Cate would accept his invitation to join them for the picnic. Not with things unsettled between them. But he hadn't exactly played fair by inviting her in front of the children. As he'd expected, they'd pleaded with her to say yes. And she found their entreaties as hard to refuse as he did.

"That would be Linda," Cate supplied. "This has her touch."

"Better hers than mine. You wouldn't want to eat anything I'd concoct." Clay gave her a rueful grin.

"You cook good," Josh said loyally. "I like your spaghetti."

"I'm glad to hear that." Chuckling, he tousled the youngster's hair. "But it's hard to go wrong with sauce from a jar."

"It's still good," Josh insisted.

Cate checked her watch. "Why don't we pack up and head down to the river? We can stake out a good spot for the fireworks and have our dessert while the band plays."

"Sounds good to me," Clay agreed.

Once everything was stowed in the cooler, Clay stood and held out a hand to Cate. After a momentary hesitation, she took it and he pulled her to her feet in one smooth, effortless motion.

"I'm sorry, Cate. I should have brought lawn chairs." He kept a firm grip on her slender fingers while she got her balance. "Sitting on the ground wasn't the best idea."

"I like picnics on the grass." She tugged her hand free and turned to brush some dried grass off Josh's bottom, avoiding eye contact with Clay.

He shoved his hands in his pockets. "I hope you like fireworks on the grass, too. We're in the same boat there."

"I'll be fine."

But half an hour later, as they chose a spot in the park by the river and he spread the blanket on the ground again, he once more regretted his oversight. Cate managed without complaint, but he knew getting up and down wasn't easy for her.

She remained on the blanket while the kids dragged him to the concession stand for ice cream cones, and when they returned she was chatting with some members of the congregation who had also gone on to the park. The steady parade of visitors continued until the sky darkened and the fireworks display began.

As he watched the bursts of color overhead, it occurred to Clay that if someone had told him six months ago what he'd be doing on this Fourth of July, he'd have laughed. He'd have been sure he'd be spending this holiday like he spent every other—alone, and probably working.

Instead, he'd gone to a religious service. Had a picnic on the lawn of a church. Conversed with countless people he hadn't known six months ago and who now considered him one of their own. He was also responsible for the two little children cuddled up beside him, their eyes wide with wonder at the dazzling display.

And then there was Cate, who'd filled his life with light as surely as the fireworks were illuminating the night sky.

Her head was tipped back as she sat beside him, her expression as enraptured as Emily's and Josh's. Her ability to find joy in simple, everyday pleasures—despite disappointments that would have turned many people cynical and bitter—was one of the things he loved about her.

Love.

The word jolted him, and for a second he stopped breathing. It was the first time he'd allowed himself to attach the L word to Cate. But he suspected the connection had been there for quite a while.

He was in love with Cate.

There was no way the Clay Adams who had arrived in Washington back in March would ever have allowed for that possibility, he acknowledged. But he'd changed over the past few months. Partly because of the children. Partly because of Cate. And partly because he'd begun to listen to the voice calling to him, inviting him to come home.

The voice of the Lord.

A passage Reverend Richards had read last week replayed in his mind. "Come to me, all you who labor and are heavy laden, and I will give you rest."

In order to accept the Lord's invitation, Clay knew he needed to put his life in God's hands. Needed to follow where He led. Like Reverend Richards, Clay now felt certain the course the Lord wanted him to follow wasn't the one he'd laid out for himself. That he was being called to start down a path with an end he couldn't see, trusting that the Lord who had brought him this far would continue to guide him.

And he at last felt ready to heed that call. Beginning right now. Because this was where he belonged. Here, in this small town, with the two children who had stolen his heart and the woman whose quiet faith, remarkable strength and simple goodness had made it beat with new life and warmth.

Repositioning himself behind Cate, he leaned close to her ear, praying she'd be receptive to this overture. He intended to honor his promise about tabling a discussion of personal matters until after the custody issue was resolved, but he wanted to begin laying the groundwork now.

"Why don't you lean on me?" He'd said the same thing to her the day she'd fallen after the kite-flying accident, he recalled. It had been an odd choice of words for a man who'd never wanted anyone to lean on him. To count on him. But he'd come through for the children. And now he felt confident he could be the kind of man Cate could lean on, and count on, too.

He gently took her shoulders, urged her back against his chest and held his breath.

Every nerve ending in Cate's body began to thrum as Clay settled behind her. When she'd accepted his invitation, she'd assumed she'd be safe, knowing the children would be effective chaperones. Yet she'd felt anything but safe all day. For one simple reason.

She'd fallen in love with the man sitting a touch away.

And she suspected his feelings were escalating as well.

So she wasn't surprised when his hands came to rest on her shoulders, nor when he whispered the invitation in her ear to lean on him.

With every ounce of her being, she wanted to do just that. It would be so easy to put her trust in him. To throw caution to the wind and give full expression to the feelings she was struggling to contain.

To get hurt.

But despite the risk, resisting him was becoming as difficult as resisting the children's innocent pleas. Except children's love was generally transparent, she reminded herself. What you saw was what you got. If they said they loved you, they did. If they offered affection, it was genuine. And unless you hurt them, their love remained strong.

Adult love, on the other hand, came with far more baggage and was far less innocent. Even if there was no intent to inflict pain, people could get hurt. She'd been there. And the experience had taught her that her disability was a double stumbling block. If Dan, a kind man of deep faith, hadn't been able to accept her limitations in the end, could she expect anyone to? Beyond that, was it fair to saddle any man for life with a woman who had her problems?

All along, she'd thought the answer to both questions was no.

But Clay was making her doubt that conclusion. He didn't appear to be put off by her disabilities. Most days he hardly seemed to notice them, accommodating her limitations with an ease that helped her forget them, too.

Yet maybe, in the long run, that effort would wear on him.

"Come on, Cate. Relax." Clay's voice spoke in her ear again as he gently massaged her stiff shoulders. "We'll reinstitute the hands-off rule tomorrow. I promise."

The temptation was too strong to resist. With a sigh of surrender, Cate leaned back.

While she felt a subtle easing of tension in his body, her reaction was the exact opposite. As she settled in against his broad chest, as she inhaled the heady scent of his masculine aftershave, as his warm breath whispered against her temple, awareness of him raced through her.

He entwined his fingers with hers, and she watched, mesmerized, as he began to stroke the back of her hand with his thumb. It was a comforting gesture in some ways, meant to reassure. But it was a prelude, too. A testing of the waters. A cautious foray into new territory.

A few minutes ago, Clay had told her to lean on him. For years Cate had struggled to prove she could make it on her own, that she didn't need to lean on anyone. But the hard truth was there were days she did need help. And would, for the rest of her life. She'd learned to accept that. Dan hadn't been able to. Would Clay ultimately come to the same conclusion?

As if sensing her doubts, Clay gave her fingers a gentle, encouraging squeeze that communicated a clear message: Trust me. All will be well.

She prayed that was true.

Chapter Fourteen

As the doorbell echoed through the house, Cate checked her watch. Pop had promised to stop by Clay's after lunch and take her and the children out for ice cream, but he was pretty early for that. Unless he was angling for a meal. An affectionate smile teased her lips as she headed for the door.

The older man on the other side was definitely not Pop, however, and her smile faded under his harsh, judgmental scrutiny.

"Who are you?" he demanded in an imperious tone.

"I'm Cate Shepard." She figured she knew the answer to her next question but asked it anyway. "Who are you?"

"Clayton Adams. The children's grandfather." He peered over Cate's shoulder.

She turned to find Josh and Emily hovering in the hall doorway, their faces anxious. She gave them a reassuring smile, but their attention was riveted on the unwelcome visitor.

"Do you live here?"

At the man's belligerent question, Cate willed herself to remain calm. Her instincts told her it would be a mistake to let this man intimidate her.

Standing straighter, she did her best to maintain a placid expression and return his look without wavering. "I watch the children during the day." She kept her inflection pleasant and eased the door toward the closed position. "I'll be happy to tell Clay you stopped by."

The man gave a dismissive snort. "I didn't come to see him. I came to see the children."

Cate lowered her voice, but her tone was firm. "I understand there's a court date soon. That might be a better time to visit."

His eyes narrowed. "I didn't come to steal the children, if that's what you're worried about, missy. I just want to check out the report from that social worker. The picture she painted of Clay didn't sound anything like the rebellious, irresponsible boy I raised. And that character reference from a minister…" He gave another derisive snort. "That's a joke. Clay hasn't darkened the door of a church in years, except for Anne's funeral."

With great difficulty, Cate held on to her temper. "First of all, Mr. Adams, the report from the social worker is accurate. Clay is one of the most responsible people I've ever met. You can see for yourself he's provided a nice house with a large yard for the children, who are happy and healthy. As for Reverend Richards—feel free to talk with him yourself, if you like. Clay is a well-respected member of the congregation. If you hoped to find any discrepancies in the social worker's report, your trip was wasted."

"Hmph." He gave her one more assessing perusal, but held his ground. "Since I drove all the way down here, I don't intend to leave without seeing the children."

Cate hesitated. She doubted whether the older man would use physical force to take Josh and Emily. Not with a court date three weeks away and matters now in the hands of lawyers and a judge. What could it hurt to let him in for a few minutes? It might even help. Maybe if he saw how happy the children were, if he realized Clay was serious about his responsibility to them, his attitude might soften. It was probably a long shot, but what did she have to lose?

"We were getting ready to have lunch. Would you like to join us?"

The older man blinked, then squinted as he appraised her.

"There's no hidden agenda, if that's what you're wondering," Cate told him in a quiet voice.

His features softened infinitesimally. "All right. I'll stay." As she moved aside, he stepped over the threshold. "Hello, Emily. Hello, Joshua."

The two children looked to Cate for guidance. She gave them a reassuring smile and placed her hands on their shoulders. "Your grandfather is going to have lunch with us. He drove all the way down from Iowa to visit. Can you say hello to him?"

Emily managed a subdued greeting, but Josh just clung harder to Cate's leg.

"I was about to put the food on the table. Come on into the kitchen." She directed her comment to Clay's father. Without waiting for a response, she guided the children toward the back of the house. After a few seconds, she heard him following. "Have a seat. I'll set another place."

As she helped Josh into the booster seat and withdrew another place setting from the utensil drawer, Clay's father remained standing, watching her.

"Are you sure you're capable of taking care of two active, young children?"

A flush warmed her cheeks at his rude question. She couldn't disguise her limp. And despite her adeptness at using her semifunctional left hand, it did take her longer to perform some chores—like setting the table.

"I've learned to cope with my disabilities," she said with quiet dignity. "And I have a background in early childhood education. I've been doing this kind of work for ten years, with no complaints."

It was clear to Cate that Emily had picked up on the critical undertone of their grandfather's remarks, because she tilted her chin in defiance, though fear continued to lurk in her eyes. "Cate's our friend. She takes care of us real good."

"She makes great cookies. And she reads us stories. And takes us to the park," Josh chimed in.

Instead of responding, Clay's father sat at the place Cate had set for him.

Cate distributed the plates of food, taking a smaller portion for herself so there would be enough for their unexpected guest. Joining the group at the table, she smiled at Josh.

"I think it's your turn today, sweetie." She bowed her head, and the children followed suit.

"Thank you, Lord, for this good food Cate cooked," Josh prayed. "And thank you for sending her to us. And thank you for Uncle Clay, who takes good care of us, too. Amen." He cast a quick, mutinous look at his grandfather.

Cate did her best to put the children at ease during the meal, but she wasn't surprised when they picked at their food. Her own appetite had vanished, too, in the uncomfortable atmosphere. As well as from the strain of trying to stay one step ahead of the older man, who alternated between throwing out questions and giving the house, the meal, the children and her a critical once-over.

However, Cate didn't think he would be able to find fault with a thing. The house was clean and tidy, and she'd been adding homey touches. There were curtains at the window in the sunny yellow kitchen, and the children's artwork adorned the refrigerator. A bouquet of fresh flowers from her garden graced the table, and a plaque that read, "Lord, please bless this house in which we dwell" hung on the wall—a gift from Reverend Richards after Clay helped with the pavilion. The lunch was nutritious and filling. The children were well-dressed, their skin had a healthy glow and they had filled out.

Yet it was obvious from the older man's questions that he was intent on finding fault. Cate felt as if she were playing dodge ball as she tried to keep up with his rapid-fire delivery and quick change of subjects.

"Do you go to church?" he asked the children.

At Cate's smile and nod, Emily responded. "Yes. We go every Sunday. That's when I talk to Mommy."

"After church Uncle Clay takes us out to a restaurant for pancakes," Josh added.

"Do you ever have any company?" the older man asked them.

"Sometimes Pop comes over."

"And that lady," Josh chimed in. "She comes once in a while."

The man's lips lifted in a humorless, gloating smile. "Does she stay all night?"

"No. She just visits. Once she came when Cate was here. Remember, Cate?"

"Yes. That would be Martha Douglas, the social worker."

The older man's face fell. But he made a quick recovery. "Your uncle has a busy job. Do you get to see him very much?"

Emily tipped her head and gave him a puzzled look. "Of course. He lives here. We see him all the time. And he fixes breakfast for us every morning."

"Oatmeal," Josh supplied.

"And sometimes eggs. Or cereal," Emily offered. "And he makes dinner for us every night. After that, he plays with us."

"We went out for ice cream last night," Josh told him.

"After we play, we have story time. Then we take a bath."

Josh made a face. "Yeah. Every night."

"And after the bath we say our prayers and he tucks us in," Emily concluded.

Though Cate was ready to step in if the questions got out of line, she was content to let the children handle most of them. They were doing fine on their own, painting an admirable—and accurate—picture of Clay. But now and then she added to their responses.

"Clay's job is very demanding, as you noted," she told his father. "It's not a typical nine-to-five position. To keep up, he often works for two or three hours here after the children go to bed."

Clayton Adams sent her a disgruntled look. It was clear he wasn't getting the kind of information he wanted.

"How did he find you?"

"At church. Clay asked our pastor to recommend someone. I was between jobs, and he suggested me."

"What church do you attend?"

Cate told him. "If you're still here on Sunday, you'd be welcome to worship there. You could meet Reverend Richards and some of Clay's friends."

Before he could respond, the front door opened. Four heads swiveled toward the living room at the sound of Clay's voice.

"I could smell Cate's chocolate chip cookies all the way to my office, so I thought I'd stop by and have my dessert with…"

At the kitchen doorway, Clay came to a dead stop. His smile faded, and his mouth settled into a grim line as he and his father locked gazes. The animosity between the two was almost tangible, as thick and suffocating as the humidity on a hot July day in Missouri.

By contrast, Clay's voice was icy. "What are you doing here?"

"I came to see the children." His father's tone was no less harsh.

Planting his fists on his hips, Clay glared at the older man. "You weren't invited."

"I don't need an invitation to see my grandchildren."

"The court will decide that."

The children's complexions had paled, and Cate took their hands. "Clay…"

At her warning note, Clay transferred his attention to the children. They had shrunk down in their chairs, eyes wide with anxiety.

Cate watched as he summoned up the facsimile of a smile and circled the table to crouch between them. "I hope you saved me some cookies."

Josh glanced at the older man and leaned closer to Clay. "We haven't had dessert yet."

"Then I'm not too late?"

"No. You can have mine. I'm not hungry anymore," Emily told him.

Clay's smile stayed in place, but it looked painted on. "No chocolate chip cookies?" He smoothed her hair back. "Are you sure you're Emily Montgomery? The girl who ate two whole doughnuts last Sunday after services? And three pancakes after that at the restaurant? That bottomless-pit Emily? Is this really you?"

"It's me." The ghost of a smile flickered at her lips.

"Are you sure you won't have a cookie with me? I came all the way home from work to have dessert with you, and it's a long walk."

That elicited a giggle. "You didn't walk. You drove your car."

"I would have walked if I didn't have a car. Just to be with you guys." He included Josh in his comment.

The little boy glowed and threw his arms around Clay's neck. Emily leaned over and planted a kiss on his cheek.

"We love you, Uncle Clay," she whispered.

"And I love you back," he murmured, his voice catching.

The older man on the other side of the table stood abruptly. "I need to be going. Thank you for lunch, Ms. Shepard. Goodbye, Joshua. Goodbye, Emily."

Clay rose as well, leaving his hands on the children's shoulders.

"Would you like to take some cookies with you?" Cate offered. "It's a long drive."

"No, thank you. I'll be in town for a couple of days."

Although his lips thinned, Clay remained silent.

When neither man moved, Cate took the initiative to break the deadlock. Rising, she headed toward the door. "I'll show you out."

For several moments Clay and his father continued to stare at each other in silence. At last the older man turned and followed her.

"Have a safe trip back," she offered.

His only response was a curt nod as he exited.

Shutting the door behind him, Cate took several slow breaths. But no relaxation technique she knew was likely to ease the knot in her stomach.

When she returned to the kitchen, Clay had refilled milk glasses and doled out cookies. He sent her a questioning glance, but at the slight shake of her head he waited until the children finished and she sent them out to the yard to play before bringing up his father's visit. Topping off his coffee, he joined her at the table.

"What happened?"

Cate propped her elbow on the table. "He showed up at the door. Said he came to see the children, and that he didn't believe the social worker's report. At first I wasn't going to let him in. But then I figured, what could it hurt? I hoped if he saw the children for a few minutes he might realize the report was accurate and that they're happy and healthy. So I invited him to lunch." She tucked her hair behind her ear and took a deep breath. "I'm sorry you were blindsided."

He grasped her hand and gave it a reassuring squeeze. "If it helped our case, it was well worth the shock. But I can't believe he would just show up like that. I think I'll call Mark and get his take on this."

As Cate cleaned up the lunch dishes, Clay placed his call. She got the gist of the exchange from his side of the conversation, but Clay filled her in after he hung up.

"Mark's going to call my father's attorney, see if he knew about this. But he doubts it. With the court date this close, he's sure the guy would never have gone along with this impromptu visit. Mark's instincts tell him my old man decided on his own to come. And that wouldn't surprise me. My father always was bullheaded once he made up his mind about something."

"He said he was staying a couple more days. Do you think he'll try to see the children again?"

"I don't know." Clay's mouth thinned. "But I'll be with them all weekend. I won't let him upset them if he does show up."

"His very presence upsets them."

"I know. It upsets me, too."

Although Cate was the one who'd enforced the hands-off rule in the past, this time she broke it, laying her hand on his arm in a gesture meant to comfort. "Prayer might be a good idea about now, Clay."

He covered her hand with his, touched by her gesture. "Believe it or not, I've been bending the Lord's ear quite a bit in the past few weeks. He may be sorry I'm finding my way back to Him."

"That's the nice thing about Him, Clay." A smiled whispered at her lips. "He never gets tired of listening. And He's always with us. We'll just have to keep praying and put our trust in Him."

As he gazed into the lovely, trusting eyes of the woman he'd come to love, Clay accepted the truth of her statement. Prayer was the only avenue open to him at this point. On a lot of issues.

Yet all at once he knew it was enough.

And with that knowledge, with that letting go, came a quiet, gentle peace unlike any he'd ever known.

Chapter Fifteen

Clayton Adams peered around the woman in the pew in front of him to check on his son and grandchildren, who were seated about halfway back from the sanctuary, on the aisle. Then his gaze shifted to Cate. She was sitting on the other side with a larger group of people. They hadn't noticed him as he'd slipped into church and taken a seat in the back, just as the service began. That was good. He wanted to observe them for a while before they became aware of his presence.

That was only one of his reasons for coming to the service, however. He'd also wanted to spend some time with the Lord. Especially after the past disturbing couple of days.

Yet his unease went farther back than that, he reflected. Back to the phone conversation with Clay months ago, when his son had accused him of causing Anne's death. Clayton had dismissed the charge as preposterous, a remark prompted by anger, designed to hurt, with no basis in fact.

As the weeks passed, however, he'd been unable to put it out of his mind. The accusation had gnawed at his gut day and night, refusing to be pushed aside. In truth, he *had* pressed Anne to stay in a marriage he'd known years ago should never have taken place. Now she was dead.

And maybe he could have prevented the tragedy.

It hurt to acknowledge that. He'd always seen things as black or white, good or bad, right or wrong. There had been no room in his life for nuances.

But Clay's accusation had shaken him. Caused him to question things. And if he'd been wrong about Anne, could he have been wrong about other things, too?

Like his son's character?

He'd told Cate he'd come to see his grandchildren. And that had been the truth. Just not the whole truth. He'd also come to see what kind of man his son had become. And everything he'd discovered had been a hundred and eighty degrees from the image he'd had in his mind all these years. Far from being the promiscuous, irresponsible vagabond Clayton had always assumed he was, Clay appeared to have become honorable, dependable and trustworthy.

Or perhaps he always had been.

That had been a shocking insight for Clayton. One that had left him feeling uncertain and off balance.

But so had something else. As he'd watched Clay interact with the children at lunch, as he watched him now, here in this church, tenderly brush Joshua's hair back from his face and rest his hand on Emily's shoulder, he realized Clay had become a father.

Perhaps a better one than he had ever been.

That acknowledgment also came hard for him. He'd never liked to admit he was wrong. That he'd failed. He'd always considered it a sign of weakness. And God disliked weakness. Or so he'd been raised to believe.

But according to the pastor at this church, that wasn't true. In his sermon, the minister had said God recognizes our humanity and loves us in spite of our mistakes, and that He always forgives us if we come to Him with true repentance.

That was a far different message than the one he heard in his own church, where the pastor talked only about punishment. In fact, this whole church experience had been unlike anything he was accustomed to. It was quieter here. Less judgmental. More loving. He could feel a sense of fellowship he'd never known in his church.

And it made him realize he had a lot of thinking to do. About a lot of things.

The congregation stood for the final hymn, and as the last verse was being sung Clayton slipped out. In a few minutes, he'd start the long drive back to Iowa. Those solitary hours in the car would give him plenty of time to think things through.

But he had one more thing to do before he headed home.

At the touch of Cate's arm on his sleeve outside church, Clay excused himself from his conversation with Pastor Bob and turned to her.

Her troubled expression, however, wiped the smile from his face. As did her slight pallor. Gripping her arms in alarm, he searched her face. "What's wrong? Are you sick?"

"No. Your father's here. On the far side of the lawn." She kept her voice low.

A muscle in Clay's jaw clenched. He'd hoped the man was long gone. Instead, according to Cate, he was steps away.

Thinking fast, Clay decided to ignore him. The children hadn't yet noticed their grandfather's presence, and he could spirit them away to see the ducks in the pond behind church. After his father's visit on Friday, it had taken hours for the kids to settle down. He didn't want them disturbed again.

As if reading his mind, Cate spoke again. "I think he's waiting to speak with you, Clay." She kept an eye on the older man. "And he's holding presents."

Presents? That was certainly out of character, Clay reflected. "I don't want to upset the children again. They feel threatened around him."

"He doesn't look threatening today. I sense there's been a change."

Cate's intuition with the kids had always been sound, and Clay had no reason to think it wouldn't translate to a situation like this. And if things *had* changed—for the better—he'd welcome the news.

Steeling himself, he turned toward his father.

The older man stood at the edge of the church lawn, holding two gaily wrapped packages. He straightened when Clay looked at him and gave a stiff nod.

"I'll see what he has to say. Can you distract the kids?" They were playing with a small group of youngsters a few yards away, still oblivious to the presence of the older man.

"Yes."

Leaving the children in Cate's care, Clay approached his father, stopping about six feet away. "Checking up on the social worker's report, I see." He made no attempt to hide his hostility.

Hot color suffused Clayton's face. "That was part of the reason I came. But I also wanted to attend services, like I do every Sunday. And Ms. Shepard invited me." He elevated the packages slightly. "I brought these for the children."

"Why?"

"I'm their grandfather. It's in the job description."

Thrown by his father's awkward attempt at humor, Clay stared at him.

"Look, I'm getting ready to head home." Clayton shifted the packages in his arms. "I'd like to say goodbye to the children. Please."

The last word came out raspy, as if it had gotten stuck in the older man's throat. Clay wasn't surprised. He couldn't remember one time in his entire life when Clayton Adams had said please.

As for presents, the ones he'd received as a child had been confined to special occasions, and they'd always been practical things. Socks. Shirts. Gloves. Clay had a niggling suspicion these gifts didn't fall into that category.

Clay debated. If the man was bearing gifts, making an effort to be nice, perhaps he should let the children talk to him. It might dispel some of the fear they harbored about their grandfather. And anything he could do to erase fear from their life was worth a try.

Turning toward Cate, he signaled for her to bring Josh and Emily over.

Thirty silent seconds passed before she joined them, a child holding each hand.

Clayton held out the packages to the children. "These are for you."

"But it's not our birthday." Emily inspected them with a puzzled expression."

"Or Christmas," Josh added.

"That's okay. It doesn't always have to be a special day to give presents."

Emily and Josh looked up at Clay, their faces uncertain but hopeful. Dredging up a smile, he nodded. "It's okay. You can take them."

They shyly reached for the packages with a murmured "thank-you."

"When you play with those, I hope you'll think about me."

Emulating his son's behavior the prior day, Clayton bent down to their level. "That's a pretty dress, Emily."

She gave him a tentative smile. "Cate helped me pick it out."

"The two of you did a fine job. It's perfect for church." He directed his next comment to Josh. "I noticed you during the service. I think you were the best-behaved boy there."

Josh's smile was less reserved than Emily's. "Uncle Clay says we have to be good when we visit God. I try real hard."

"Well, you did a good job."

"We're going to get pancakes," Josh told him. "Do you want to come?"

The older man blinked. Cleared his throat. Sniffed. "I'm afraid I can't today. I'm going home now, and it's a long drive back to Iowa. But thank you very much for asking."

He stood, and once more his eyes were almost level with Clay's. "I'll be in touch."

With that, he turned and walked toward his car.

"Can we open these, Uncle Clay?"

At Emily's eager question, Clay cast a distracted glance in her direction. "Sure."

The two children tore into the packages, shrieking with glee at the doll and toy keyboard that emerged from the wrapping paper.

As they examined their gifts, Clay drew Cate aside. "What do you make of this?"

"I'm not sure. It was like he was trying to make amends."

He shook his head. "I don't trust him."

"Trust is a very hard thing to reestablish once it's broken."

Her wistful tone, which suggested her remark encompassed more than his relationship with his father, redirected Clay's thoughts to the woman beside him. Pop had told him weeks ago

Cate had been hurt by Dan Maxwell. If her former beau had betrayed her trust, it was no wonder she shied away from relationships. While dealing with that issue was high on his agenda once the custody situtation was resolved, he intended to try and continue to lay some groundwork in the meantime, as he had on Fourth of July.

"Will you join us for breakfast today, Cate?" He'd asked before, but she'd always turned him down. So today he added a caveat. "It would make the kids happy." He held out his hand, his gaze locked on hers. "Me, too."

She hesitated for an instant, then slipped her fingers in his. "Yes."

In Cate's soft assent, Clay heard more than a mere agreement to accompany them to the local diner. He sensed it had been a "yes" to much more. And as they gathered up the children and headed for his truck, he relished the feel of their linked hands— and gave thanks for that blessing.

As for the situation with his father…he knew Cate had been praying for a positive outcome. As had he. But what he'd had in mind was a ruling in his favor from the judge. He hadn't expected his father's hard-line attitude to change. Yet everything the old man had done today had been out of character. He had been like a different person.

Weeks ago, when the children had added prayers for their grandfather to their bedtime talk with God, Clay recalled thinking it would take a miracle to soften the heart of his father.

But maybe—just maybe—God had, indeed, worked that miracle.

Two days later, Clay's cell phone began to vibrate as he examined a crack in the foundation of the new plant. Distracted, he unclipped it from his belt and pressed it to his ear. "Hello."

"Clay, it's Becky. Mark Shepard called. He says it's urgent. Do you want his number?"

The crack in the concrete fell to the bottom of his priority list. "Yeah, thanks."

Becky recited the number, and Clay punched it in as he strode away from the noisy construction site. Mark's secretary put Clay through at once after he identified himself.

"Clay? I finally connected with your father's attorney. He's been in court for two days. As I suspected, he didn't know about the impromptu trip. But I have good news. Your father has agreed to withdraw his petition for custody in exchange for visiting privileges."

With all the background noise, Clay wasn't sure he'd heard Mark's message correctly. "Did you say my father is going to let me keep the children?"

"That's right. According to his attorney, he had a change of heart after his visit last weekend. He'd like you to call him to work out some arrangements."

The unexpected turn of events left Clay stunned—and speechless.

"Clay? Are you there?"

"Yeah. Yeah, I'm here. I don't get this. Why would he withdraw his petition?"

"Beats me. And his attorney couldn't offer much of an explanation. All he said was your father changed his mind."

Elation surged through Clay, but he did his best to rein it in. Until the matter was resolved once and for all, he wouldn't take anything for granted. "What happens now?"

"If you're willing to grant visiting privileges, it's over. It becomes a family issue, not a legal matter, and you and your father can work out the details."

"In other words, I have to agree to let him see the children."

"That's the stipulation. And it's not an unreasonable request, Clay. My advice is to talk to him about it, see if you can come to some agreement. If you don't, I doubt the court will be as favorable toward your case."

From the beginning, Clay had wanted to protect the children from his father. Yet his resolution had wavered after last Sunday. The old man's thinking and attitude appeared to have undergone some sort of fundamental shift.

"Can't this be arranged through you and his attorney?" Clay asked.

"No. Your father was very specific. He said he wanted to talk with you."

No surprise there. The old man had always liked to do things his way. "Okay, I'll give him a call and see what we can work out."

"Great. Let me know how it goes. We're on the docket, so if necessary we can still pay a visit to the judge. But it will be a whole lot easier on the kids if the two of you can come to some sort of agreement."

Clay didn't doubt that. He just hoped the old man would be reasonable.

And if he wasn't, Clay intended to keep that court date.

After reassuring himself Josh and Emily were asleep, Clay eased their bedroom door shut and headed toward the kitchen. It was time to place the call.

He'd been thinking about it all day. And dreading it. He and his father had never communicated well, even about unimportant things. They were bound to clash on a topic of this magnitude. But he was willing to try, for the sake of the children.

As he sat at the kitchen table and picked up the phone, Clay noted without surprise that his hands were trembling. Considering all that was at stake, he wanted the discussion to go well. But it had been years since he and his father had had a civil conversation. Or tried to. This was going to be awkward. And challenging.

After weighing the phone in his hand for another minute, Clay forced himself to punch in his father's number. There was no sense delaying the inevitable.

His father answered on the second ring, as if he'd been sitting by the phone. "Hello."

Clay dispensed with a greeting and got straight to the point. "My attorney said you wanted to speak with me."

There was a brief silence on the other end. "I wasn't sure you'd call."

"My attorney advised me to. I just want what's best for the children."

"So do I." Again there was a slight pause, and Clay heard his father take a deep breath. "And I think the best thing for them is to stay with you."

"That's not what you thought when you filed for custody."

"I've learned a few things since then. And discovered I've made some mistakes."

Clay had no idea how to respond. As far back as he could remember, his father had never admitted to being wrong about anything.

As if aware of Clay's dilemma, the older man gave a mirthless chuckle. "I guess I shouldn't be surprised by your reaction. I've been pretty hard-nosed and self-righteous all my life. Too much so, I guess. I realized that after you blamed me for Anne's death. I resented your comment, but over the past few weeks I've come to accept you were right. If I hadn't been adamant with her about honoring her marriage vows, she'd still be with us."

A brief pang of regret echoed in Clay's heart at his father's words. He'd thrown out that accusation in anger—and without full information. After talking with Pop about his wife, Clay had come to understand that in all likelihood Anne had been held to Martin by many strings she'd never revealed to him. Reluctance to face their father's disapproval had been one of them. But only one.

"I shouldn't have said that." Clay forced out the words. He wasn't good at admitting he was wrong, either. At least to his old man. "Battered women stay in those situations for a lot of reasons. What you said to Anne didn't help, but I'm sure it wasn't the only reason she stuck with him."

"Some of the blame is mine, though. And I started thinking that if I was wrong about that, I might be wrong about other things. Including my son. As I discovered last weekend, I was." He cleared his throat. "I learned something else, too, as I watched you with Joshua and Emily. You're a better father than I ever was. I never had your parenting skills. But I'm going to work on them. I failed with you and Anne, but I want a second chance with Joshua and Emily. That's why I requested visiting privileges. In whatever form you're willing to grant them."

Clay tried to assimilate everything his father had said. It was so unexpected, so against type, he was beginning to doubt the man on the other end of the line was Clayton Adams. His father never asked. He demanded. And he'd always had to be in control. Yet he was leaving the arrangements in Clay's hands with a promise to abide by whatever terms his son offered.

Despite that positive development, however, there was still a lot of baggage to deal with. The memories of his unhappy childhood left a bitter taste in Clay's mouth, and he didn't know how he could get past that. Or *if* he could. Reverend Richards often talked about the importance of forgiveness, and Clay knew this was the biggest test he'd ever face. But he wasn't sure he was up to the task.

All at once, the encounter with his father on the church lawn last Sunday replayed in his mind. The kids had been cautious at first. But after the older man had gotten down on their level and talked to them in a kind voice, Josh had warmed to him, even inviting him for breakfast. The little boy had been willing to let go of past hurts and give the man another chance.

Perhaps that was the example Clay should follow.

It wouldn't be as fast or as easy for him as it had been for Josh. There was too much painful history between him and his father. But maybe, with the Lord's help, he could find a way to take the first steps on a new path with his father. To give their relationships one more chance.

"All I'm asking for is a chance, Clay."

His father's words, strained and worried, so closely mirrored Clay's thoughts that he couldn't write them off as mere coincidence. Making his decision, he tightened his grip on the phone and took the plunge.

"All right. Let's give it a try."

Cate had been sitting by her phone trying to balance her checkbook for the past half hour, but the numbers wouldn't add up. Thanks to her distraction, not her math skills. She might as well give it up until Clay called with a report on his conversation with his father, as he'd promised he would, she conceded.

When the phone trilled at last, she lunged for it, fumbled, and watched in dismay as it fell to the floor. Spinning across the tile, it went silent.

Great. She'd probably broken it, Cate berated herself in disgust as she scrambled off the stool at the counter and went to retrieve it.

Before she managed to pick it up, however, it began to ring again.

This time, she clamped her good hand around it and pressed it firmly against her ear. "Hello?"

A chuckle came over the line. "I've had women hang up on me in the past, but not before I say hello."

Clay's relaxed, upbeat tone told her all she needed to know. Her shoulders sagged in relief as she sank back onto the stool. "It went well?"

"Very." He gave her a recap, ending with his father's willingness to let him set the visitation schedule. "The outcome is about as good as I could have hoped. And now we need to celebrate. How about dinner Thursday night?"

"Sure. The kid's will love a party."

"*Their* party is tomorrow night. I'm bringing pizza home. You're welcome to join us then, too, but Thursday is for you and me. We deserve a night out after all the stress of the past few months."

He was asking her out on a date.

As the implication sank in, Cate's pulse tripped into double time. Clay had promised not to bring up personal issues until the custody issue was resolved, and he'd been good about that—even if both of them had slipped on the hands-off rule. But she hadn't expected him to jump on this so soon.

Then again, Clay wasn't the kind of person who put things off. If a need arose, he addressed it. That's how he'd been with the children—always on top of issues, doing his best to resolve them. She should have expected him to confront the problems in their relationship the instant he was able.

She just wasn't sure he could solve them.

Not that there was any doubt in her mind about her feelings— or Clay's. She loved him, and she was pretty sure he loved her. He might not yet be ready to make a commitment, but it was obvious he was headed in that direction. The short-term looked rosy.

The long-term was what worried her. When the moment of truth came, would he follow through—or back out, as Dan had? And suppose he did take the plunge into matrimony—only to decide down the road that living with a disabled woman wasn't worth the effort?

Those were the concerns that had disrupted her sleep for the past few weeks. She could lay them out to Clay, but no matter what assurances he gave her, there were no guarantees. And it wasn't only her emotional wellbeing that was at stake. Two little children, who had already endured too much trauma in their short lives, would also be devastated if she and Clay connected, only to have things fall apart later.

"Hey, Cate. Loosen up. It's just a dinner." His teasing tone interrupted her internal debate. "If you don't want to talk about us, we'll defer that discussion to another night. But come with me. I have a lot to be thankful for, and I'd like to celebrate with you."

How could she refuse a request like that? Besides, they had to talk sooner or later. It might as well be sooner. "Okay, Clay. It's a date."

"Great!" The word was filled with relief—and elation. "And get all gussied up. We're doing this in style."

Chapter Sixteen

"Mmm! That was a great meal!" Cate smiled and leaned back in her chair at Washington's upscale riverside restaurant. The oppressive July heat had abated enough to allow for patio dining, and the flickering candles on the tables bathed the scene in soft illumination.

"I'm glad you liked it." Clay gave her a lazy smile as he took a sip of his after-dinner coffee, admiring the shimmer of her blond hair and the golden glow of her complexion in the candlelight. She looked beautiful in a sleeveless silk dress, the beaded round neckline dipping to reveal a hint of creamy skin below her collarbone. A flat gold necklace glinted with every breath she took, directing his attention to the delicate hollow of her throat.

He was grateful she'd relaxed as the evening progressed. When he'd picked her up, she'd been taut as a plumb line. But true to his word, he'd steered the conversation away from personal topics. And the great meal, tranquil ambience and easy conversation had mellowed her out. She looked comfortable, content—and very, very appealing.

"I should never have eaten that whole piece of Mississippi

mud pie." Cate groaned. "I'll be paying for those calories for a week. Chocolate goes right to my hips."

"Not that I've noticed." He gave her an unrepentant grin.

She blushed and tucked her hair behind her ear. "It's true, though. One of my favorite treats growing up was a fudgesicle. But when I was dancing, I only allowed myself one a week—and in lieu of dinner, at that. The weight requirements for balle-rinas are very stringent." She swiped up one last crumb of cake with her fork and popped it in her mouth. "That's one of the pluses of my current life. I can indulge in Mississippi mud pie or fudgesicles a little more often without quite as much guilt."

Since she'd brought up her past, Clay decided the subject was fair game. And perhaps it would lead to other personal topics.

"So what drew you to dancing?"

Her face grew luminous. "The oneness with the music. It was the most amazing experience."

Clay wished he could give her back the dream that had meant so much to her. But that was beyond his power. All he could hope to do was offer her a new dream.

"From what I've read, dancers don't have much of a life."

She propped her elbow on the table and rested her chin in her hand. "That's true. Dance is a hard taskmaster. You lead a pretty solitary existence focused on practice and performing."

"Considering your close family, I'm surprised that appealed to you. I would have thought you'd want a family of your own."

A flicker of distress echoed in the depths of her eyes, and she took a sip of water before responding. "I did. I'd planned to perform for ten or fifteen years, then open a dance studio. I'd expected to be married and settled down with a family by the time I was in my late thirties. Still dancing, but on my terms."

"It's not too late for the family part."

She regarded him across the flickering flame, and her profound sadness reached deep into his soul. "I gave up that dream, too."

"Because of Dan?"

She blinked. "How do you know about Dan?"

"I asked Pop who he was at the pavilion raising."

"Why?"

"I felt strange vibes the day you and he talked after church weeks ago. And I sensed Pop didn't like him either."

She cast her eyes down and toyed with her water glass. "What did Pop say?"

"That you and Dan had been serious, and the whole family expected an engagement announcement. Then one day it was over. No one knew why."

Cate traced the condensation on her glass with a fingertip. "It just didn't work out."

Clay wanted to know why. But he asked the more important question first. "Are you still in love with him?"

She hesitated, as if debating whether she should respond to his quiet query. To his relief, she did. "No. To be honest, I've begun to wonder if I ever really was. I think maybe I just loved what he represented. He's a good Christian man who I thought was going to offer me the kind of life I've always dreamed of—a loving husband, children at my table, a stable, God-centered home."

"What happened?"

She took a deep breath and leveled a direct look at him. "My disabilities aren't always easy to cope with, Clay. There are days I need extra help. When I have to use my cane. When I can't keep up. Dan's very athletic. He loves to ski and hike and bicycle. I couldn't share those kinds of activities with him. And he felt guilty about leaving me behind to do them. After a while, that wears on a relationship."

"There's more to marriage than skiing and hiking together."

"That wasn't the only stumbling block. A lot of people are uncomfortable with disabilities. They don't like the attention they draw, or the inconvenience they cause. I've encountered plenty of people over the past fourteen years who had difficulty dealing with disabled individuals."

She scanned the patio, filled with tables of diners enjoying their meals. "Didn't you notice the attention we drew tonight as we walked in? Most people tried to be discreet, but I could feel their scrutiny. And I saw the quick, embarrassed way they averted their eyes if I caught them watching me. That happens wherever I go."

If their entrance had drawn attention, Clay hadn't been aware of it. He'd been too focused on the lovely woman across from him. "If Dan had a problem with that, how did you two ever get serious?"

She shrugged. "I guess I ignored the signs. Dan used to tell me he prayed every day for my healing. Even after I explained that the doctors had said I'd recovered as much as I was going to, he insisted that with trust in God, anything is possible. Including miracles. I believe in miracles, but I'd come to the conclusion that for whatever reason, God has given me this cross to bear for the rest of my life. Dan didn't accept that, though. He kept praying."

Cate looked out over the wide, deep river flowing by, steady and placid, on the other side of the road. "To make a long story short, in the end he was forced to accept that I wasn't going to improve. I knew he'd been praying for me to recover. But I'd never realized his love was contingent on my recovery. Until the night he told me that while he cared for me, and knew my physical disabilities shouldn't affect the way he felt, they did."

A shaft of pain darted through her eyes and her voice grew softer. "In hindsight, I have a feeling he latched on to me out of some misplaced sense of Christian duty. That I became sort of a cause for him. Maybe he felt it was a magnanimous gesture to date a disabled woman. A demonstration of his Christian charity. And I think he believed his prayers would produce results." She lifted one shoulder. "I can't say for sure what his motivations were, but I do know he never meant to hurt me. He felt so guilty the night he broke things off that I ended up consoling *him*."

A humorless smile, whispered at the corners of her mouth. "Anyway, that experience was a wake-up call. While God loves us all, and values us the same despite our faults or disabilities, it's harder for humans to overlook the kind of problems I have. They're often inconvenient, sometimes embarrassing and, to varying degrees, limiting. Much as I hate to admit it, there are days I'm not up to taking a walk, let alone engaging in sports. A lot of people don't want to deal with that for the rest of their lives. Dan was one of them."

Clay regarded the sweet, gentle, caring woman across from him—and had some very unchristian thoughts about the man who had hurt her. "Do you know what I think, Cate?"

Her expression became guarded. "What?"

"I think Dan was an idiot. And that's the nicest thing I can say about him."

Clay saw hope flicker to life in Cate's deep green eyes. But it was tempered by caution that had been forged from disappointment and pain and experience. Before this night was over, however, he intended to put her fears to rest.

Removing his napkin from his lap, he set it on the table. "Are you finished with your coffee?"

"Yes."

He scanned the check the waiter had left a few minutes ago, removed some bills from his wallet and tossed them on the table. "Let's continue this discussion over there, in privacy." He gestured toward the benches spaced along the riverbank, none of which were occupied on this warm evening.

Five minutes later, seated side by side, he smiled at her. "Much better. Now where were we?"

She tipped her head. "I thought we weren't going to get into a personal discussion tonight."

"It just came up naturally." He rested one elbow on the back of the bench, his fingers brushing her arm. "We can defer it until tomorrow, though, if you prefer."

With a sigh, she shook her head. "I guess we might as well continue. There's no sense putting off the inevitable."

"My thoughts exactly." He extended his hand toward her. "I have a few things to say, and I'd like to hold your hand while I do that."

She considered his long, lean, sun-browned fingers. When at last she lifted her right hand, he shook his head and retracted his.

"The other one, Cate." His tone was gentle, coaxing. "Trust me on this, okay?"

He saw the conflict in her eyes. The uncertainty. The yearning. He prayed the latter would win out.

It did. A few moments later, she lifted her left hand and placed it in his.

Gratified by her trust, Clay traced each finger with a gentle, unhurried touch. "You have beautiful hands, Cate. Both of them."

"This one doesn't work very well, though." Her voice caught on the last word.

"True. But something much more important works perfectly. Your heart." He leaned forward, willing her to hear the truth in his words as he cradled her hands in his. "I'll admit that the first thing I noticed the day we met was your limp. And your hand. I remember wondering what had happened to someone so young and beautiful to cause such disabilities. I guess I fell into the curious camp that day.

"But the funny thing is, the longer I knew you, the less I noticed your disabilities. There were too many other, more important, things to notice. Your kindness. Your tender heart. Your gentle way with the children. Your deep faith. Your devotion to your family. Your consideration and empathy and generous spirit. I discovered you were smart and strong and wise beyond your years.

"I know this might sound strange, Cate, but I don't think your disabilities are a burden at all. I think they're a gift that has led you to travel a better path than the one you planned."

Jolted, Cate stared at Clay. Through the years, she'd viewed her disabilities in many ways. As a problem. An affliction. A cross. But never as a gift. How could the burden that had robbed her of her dreams and almost destroyed her life be a gift? Even after she'd accepted her limitations, she'd never thought of them in such positive terms.

Yet Clay might be right, she acknowledged. She had learned and grown and matured as a result of her illness. And while she'd given up the dream that had guided her youth, she'd found a different, very satisfying life. One that had led her to this place, this time, this man. If her dreams of being a ballerina had come true, she'd never have met Clay. Perhaps never had the opportunity to consider marriage or a family as she juggled the demands and rigors demanded by the life of a dancer.

And as she got lost in Clay's warm, adoring eyes, the last of her doubts dissolved. If Dan had convinced her that taking a chance on commitment was risky due to her disabilities, Clay had convinced her by his words, his touch, his actions that if love was real, her disabilities posed no risk at all. That, in fact, he considered them a blessing, because they had brought them together.

Before she could absorb all Clay had said, he slid off the bench to one knee and cocooned her hands in his. "Okay, here comes the scary part. For me, anyway." He flashed her a nervous grin, then grew serious again. "Over the past few months, thanks to you and your family, I've come to realize that a good marriage and a loving family don't tie you down. They lift you up. That they're not a burden, but a gift to be cherished. The secret, I think, is finding the right woman. And I found her in you."

His compelling gaze held hers, and he swallowed hard. "Cate Shepard, I love you. Would you do me the honor of becoming my wife?"

A single tear tracked down Cate's cheek, and when Clay reached up to brush it away she covered his unsteady hand with hers, pressing it against her cheek.

"I love you, too, Clay Adams. I never thought I'd risk saying that again. But I'm not afraid with you. I trust you with my life—and with my heart. And I want to be with you for always. So yes. I would be honored to become your wife."

At the elation, the radiant joy, that swept over his face, Cate's throat constricted with tenderness. And when he drew her to her feet, pulled her into his arms and lowered his mouth to hers, she surrendered to the warm kiss that was filled with promise.

When at last he released her lips, she clung to the lapels of his charcoal gray suit, resting in the shelter of his strong arms. Trying to convince herself this was real. But the thudding of his heart against her ear, the spicy scent of his aftershave, proved that this moment wasn't just some romantic fantasy she'd conjured up in her imagination. It really was happening.

And best of all, it was only the beginning.

Clay eased back at last, but he kept her in the circle of his arms as his tender gaze traced every nuance of her face. "I've never asked a woman to marry me before. Is there some sort of protocol I should follow? Do guys still ask fathers for their daughter's hand?"

Cate smiled up at him, and her heart overflowed with joy. "You don't need to talk to Dad. But why don't we ask the children?"

"Is this Saturday?" Josh rubbed his eyes as he and Emily wandered into the kitchen the next morning, brightening at the cinnamon rolls on the counter.

"No. It's Friday," Clay replied.

"Then how come you didn't go to work today?"

"It's a special occasion."

Emily tilted her head. "Is it a holiday? Like the Fourth of July?"

"In a way."

"Will there be fireworks?" Josh was growing more interested by the second.

"Yes. But only in my heart." Before they could ask any more questions, Clay changed the subject. "Did you have fun with Pop last night?"

"Yeah. He read us two stories and we sang songs and went outside and caught lightning bugs. He said we were having a…a…"

"…a slumber party," Emily finished. "Is Cate coming over today?"

The doorbell rang, and Clay grinned. "That's her now. Wash your hands and we'll have breakfast in a few minutes."

Stifling a yawn, Clay strode toward the front door. He hoped Cate didn't want a long engagement. Too wired to sleep after the life-changing step they'd taken last night, he'd ended up reading an old engineering book until boredom lulled him into a restless slumber. He doubted he was going to get a decent night's sleep until they were married.

Pulling open the front door, he drank in the sight of the woman he loved. Backlit by the morning sun, Cate's hair resembled a halo and her eyes were luminous.

She tilted her head and smiled at him as she stepped over the threshold. "You seem happy."

"That's because I'm thinking about this." He leaned over and claimed her lips in a lingering kiss, leaving one hand on the doorknob while the other played with her silky hair.

The kiss went on longer than he'd planned…until childish giggles interrupted them. Releasing Cate's lips with reluctance, he checked out the kids over his shoulder.

Emily and Josh stood a few feet away in the living room, watching the scene with avid interest—and obvious approval.

"You guys kiss like the people on TV," Emily said, alerting Clay he'd have to do a better job monitoring their television viewing.

"You kiss good," Josh added, not about to be left out of the discussion.

Clay chuckled. "Listen, why don't you two come into the living room for a minute? We have something to tell you." Closing the door, he linked his hand with Cate's and led her to the couch. As they sat, the children clambered up beside them, one on each side.

As Clay opened his mouth, planning to lead up to the news slowly, Emily spoke. "Are you guys going to get married?"

Clay closed his mouth.

"We'd like to," Cate stepped in. "What do you two think about that?"

Josh considered it. "Would we all get to live together, like a real family?"

"Yes."

"Would you be our new mommy and daddy? Like that girl you knew, who was adopted?" Emily asked.

When Cate hesitated, Clay took over. "Would you like that?"

"I'd like you to be our daddy. But…" Emily wrinkled her brow. "We have a mommy already, in heaven."

"She'll always be your mommy, sweetheart." Cate took the little girl's hand, brushing a wisp of hair back from her forehead. "And she'll always love you. I would just take her place here on earth, since she can't be with you again until you go to heaven."

"I think that's a real good idea," Josh said.

"Me, too," Emily concurred. "I think Mommy would want someone to help Uncle Clay. And I don't think he could find anyone better than you."

"I agree," Clay responded in a husky, tender tone designed to communicate to Cate just how much he loved and cherished her.

Josh tipped his head and looked at Cate. "Do you have fireworks in your heart, too?"

When it took Cate a moment to disengage from his gaze, he figured his message had gotten through loud and clear. "What do you mean, sweetie?"

"Before you came this morning, Uncle Clay said today was a holiday, like the Fourth of July. Except he said the fireworks were in his heart. You kind of look like you have fireworks in your heart, too."

Cate once more turned to Clay, her face aglow with joy. "I do."

"Do you remember the time you were reading us a book, and I asked if happily-ever-after really happened, or if it was just in stories?" Emily asked.

"I remember," Cate said.

"I guess it does. Because I think this is a happily-ever-after, don't you?"

Clay smiled at Cate. The love shining in her eyes told him her answer to Emily's question. And it matched his. Both of them had made a long journey. In God's time, their paths had intersected. And with His grace, they'd found the courage to join hands and continue the journey together. Taking two very special children along.

"Yes, Emily." The love in his heart overflowed, filling him with a sustaining warmth as gentle and life-giving as spring sunshine. "I would say this is definitely a happily-ever-after."

Epilogue

Eighteen Months Later

"**Y**ou know, two big events in the same month wasn't our best idea." Cate tossed the comment over her shoulder to Clay as she dug through one of the boxes piled around the bedroom in their new home.

"Who knew the perfect house would come on the market at exactly the wrong time? You aren't sorry we bought it, are you?"

"No. But I'm a little amused by God's timing."

"I'm glad you've kept your sense of humor through all of this. That's one of the things I love about you."

He touched her cheek, and the warmth and contentment in his eyes sent Cate's heart soaring.

"When are we going?" Emily burst into the room with Josh in tow.

"So much for privacy," Clay murmured to Cate with a wink.

But neither of them would have it any other way, she knew. While she'd never planned on inheriting a ready-made family, and Clay hadn't planned on any family at all, Josh and Emily filled their days with so much joy it was impossible to imagine their life without the children.

"As soon as Uncle Clay finds the blanket," Cate told them. Grinning, she gestured to the boxes. "You're on your own, dear husband. I have other things to attend to."

When she reappeared a few minutes later, Clay held up the white satin, hand-embroidered coverlet in triumph. "Ta da!"

"Thank goodness! Mom would have been devastated if we hadn't found it."

She eased herself onto the bed, lowering the bundle in her arms to give the children a better view. Clay was right behind them, and Cate's throat tightened at his tender expression as he gave the newest member of their family his full attention.

Benjamin Clayton Adams stared back at the four faces above him with solemn brown eyes as dark as his father's, taking all the attention in stride. He looked—and acted—regal, in the heirloom christening gown that had been in the Shepard family for three generations.

"Hang in there, big fella." Clay stroked the baby's porcelain skin with one finger. "You'll get your moment in the spotlight soon."

Benjamin emitted a soft coo and smiled, waving his fists in the air.

"He certainly knows the sound of his father's voice," Cate said.

"Yeah. I guess he does." Clay cleared his throat. "Okay, gang, let's get this show on the road. We don't want to be late."

Everyone was waiting when they arrived at the church. Reverend Richards greeted them, then led the way to the baptismal font as the assembled guests gathered around.

As the minister began the brief service, Cate did a quick survey of the group of family and friends who had come together to celebrate the joyous occasion. Her mom and dad were front and center as the proud grandparents. Beside them, Pop gave her a wink and a thumbs-up. Godparents Mark and Michelle, who were expecting again, kept an eye on their firstborn; Timmy was already adept at getting into anything and everything. Rob, who was going on duty later in the afternoon, looked handsome and very official in his uniform as he corralled the toddler. A few close family friends had been invited as well.

And off to one side, but near enough to be part of the group, stood Clayton Adams. He and Clay had reached a tentative peace, and the older man attended any family gatherings to which he was invited. Cate knew it would take a long while for father and son to get past the years of hurt between them. But she prayed for them every day, confident that in time God's healing grace would fill their hearts.

Josh and Emily, who stood close beside her, had changed the most—at least in appearance. They'd both grown several inches since she'd met them two years ago outside this very church. Gone were the anxious, traumatized looks they'd worn in those early days. Thanks to Clay's willingness to fight for their happiness, they were now cheerful, well-adjusted children.

Finally, her gaze came to rest on Clay as he smiled at his new son. With selflessness, courage and love, he'd accepted the challenge God had set before him and given two lost little children new hope and new life. Just as he had done for her.

Sensing her scrutiny, Clay smiled at Cate. She was beautiful every day, he thought, but today she looked radiant. And angelic.

In truth, he didn't think that description was a stretch. In many ways, she was a gift from God. Until she'd come along, he'd been drifting like a ship without a rudder—or an anchor. He'd been moving through life, not living it. It had taken Cate, with her courage and strength and tremendous capacity to love, to show him that commitments and relationships and love didn't hold you back. They gave you a reason to go forward.

As the minister spoke the beautiful words of the baptismal rite, reminding them of the transforming power of God's miraculous love, Clay knew he, too, had been transformed by that same love. For nothing short of a miracle would have brought him home to the Lord. Or forged a reconciliation with his father. Or given him the courage to open his heart to love.

And so, as he reached for Cate's hand and entwined his fingers with hers, he gave thanks.

For one more chance.

And for happily-ever-afters.

* * * * *

Dear Reader,

This book started life as a romantic suspense novel. But it became clear to me early on that the suspense element distracted from the gripping story of Clay's emotional journey toward faith, family and love. So after some revisions, APPRENTICE FATHER was born. The final product touched my heart, and I hope it touches yours.

To learn more about my books, I invite you to visit my Web site at www.irenehannon.com. And please watch for my new Nantucket-based Steeple Hill series, Lighthouse Lane, beginning this May with TIDES OF HOPE.

In the meantime, I wish all of you a spring filled with hope and promise. Like Clay, may you always be open to the "one more chance" the Lord offers each of us with the dawn of every new day.

Irene Hannon

QUESTIONS FOR DISCUSSION

1. In *Apprentice Father,* Clay decides to put the interests of the children above his own—a choice that radically alters his life. Have you ever been faced with a decision that required sacrifice on your part? What did you decide? Why?

2. When Josh and Emily first enter Clay's life, he doesn't think he's qualified to care for them. Yet early on, he displays behavior that suggests otherwise. Describe some of the things he does in the first fifty pages of the book that show his caring nature.

3. When Clay's sister dies he blames his father, who pressured her to stay in an abusive marriage. Yet, there are many reasons women remain in bad relationships. Do you know of anyone in an abusive relationship? Why is the person staying? What can you do to help in a situation like that?

4. Cate is jilted by the man she loves because of her disabilities. In a society that idealizes physical perfection, it can be difficult to look past appearances. Have you ever been rejected—or judged—because of your appearance? How did you handle it? How can we do a better job valuing people for what is inside rather than outside? What does the Bible teach in this regard?

5. When the book begins, Josh and Emily are traumatized. How does their behavior reflect their ordeal and the home

environment in which they lived? What are the most important things Clay and Cate do to help them recover? Do you think their experiences will affect them long-term? If so, how?

6. Clay and his father have been alienated for many years. Was the estrangement justified? What could each of them have done to heal the rift sooner? Are you estranged from anyone in your life? Can you think of some ways to bridge the gap? What keeps you from making an overture to that person?

7. Cate's quiet faith and Clay's experience at the church he attends alter his view of Christianity. What did he discover that helped him find his way back to the Lord?

8. Cate comes from a large and loving family that welcomes Clay and the children into its fold. Yet belonging—whether to a church or a family—makes Clay nervous. Why? What does he learn that helps him overcome his aversion to commitments?

9. Despite the loss of her dreams, Cate goes on to find a new life. Yet she admits that her faith faltered in the face of adversity. Have you ever had a setback that shook your faith? In what way? How did you find your way back to the Lord?

10. Why is Clay so touched by the children's Father's Day gifts? Talk about the best gift you ever received and why it was special. What does the gift of salvation teach us about the attributes of a good gift?

11. According to Pop, roots are anchors that allow a plant to grow strong enough to withstand any storm. In the beginning of the book, Clay thinks of roots as chains. How do you view roots? Why? How have your roots played a role in making you the person you are?

*Turn the page for a sneak peek of RITA® Award-winner
Linda Goodnight's heartwarming story,
HOME TO CROSSROADS RANCH.
On sale in March 2009
from Steeple Hill Love Inspired®.*

Chapter One

Nate Del Rio heard screams the minute he stepped out of his Ford F-150 SuperCrew and started up the flower-lined sidewalk leading to Rainy Jernagen's house. He double-checked the address scribbled on the back of a bill for horse feed. Sure enough, this was the place.

Adjusting his Stetson against a gust of March wind, he rang the doorbell, expecting the noise to subside. It didn't.

Somewhere inside the modest, tidy-looking brick house, at least two kids were screaming their heads off in what sounded to his experienced ears like fits of temper. A television blasted out Saturday morning cartoons—SpongeBob, he thought, though he was no expert on kids' television programs.

He punched the doorbell again. Instead of the expected *ding-dong*, a raucous alternative Christian rock band added a few more decibels to the noise level.

Nate shifted the toolbox to his opposite hand and considered running for his life while he had the chance.

Too late. The bright red door whipped open. Nate's mouth fell open with it.

When the men's ministry coordinator from Bible Fellowship had called him, he'd somehow gotten the impression that he was coming to help a little old school teacher. You know, the kind that only drives to school and church and has a big, fat cat.

Not so. The woman standing before him with taffy-blond hair sprouting out from a disheveled ponytail couldn't possibly be any older than his own thirty-one years. A big blotch of something purple stained the front of her white sweatshirt and she was bare-footed. Plus, she had a crying baby on each hip and a little red-haired girl hanging on one leg, bawling like a sick calf. And there wasn't a cat in sight.

What had he gotten himself into?

"May I help you?" she asked over the racket. Her blue-gray eyes were little too unfocused and bewildered for his comfort.

Raising his voice, he asked, "Are you Ms. Jernagen?"

"Yes," she said cautiously. "I'm Rainy Jernagen. And you are….?"

"Nate Del Rio."

She blinked, uncomprehending, all the while jiggling both babies up and down. One grabbed a hank of her hair. She flinched, her head angling to one side as she said, still cautiously, "Okaaay."

Nate reached out and untwined the baby's sticky fingers.

A relieved smile rewarded him. "Thanks. Is there something I can help you with?"

He hefted the red toolbox to chest level so she could see it. "From the Handy Man Ministry. Jack Martin called. Said you had a washer problem."

Understanding dawned. "Oh, my goodness. Yes. I'm so sorry. You aren't what I expected. Please forgive me."

She wasn't what he expected either. Not in the least. Young and with a houseful of kids. He suppressed a shiver. No wonder she looked like the north end of a southbound cow. Kids, even grown ones, could drive a person to distraction. He should know. His adult sister and brother were, at this moment, making his life as miserable as possible. The worst part was they did it all the time. Only this morning his sister, Janine, had finally packed up and gone back to Sal, giving Nate a few days' reprieve.

"Come in, come in," the woman was saying. "It's been a crazy morning what with the babies showing up at three a.m. and Katie having a sick stomach. Then while I was doing the laundry, the washing machine went crazy. Water everywhere." She jerked her chin toward the inside of the house. "You're truly a godsend."

He wasn't so sure about that, but he'd signed up for his church's ministry to help single women and the elderly with those pesky little handyman chores like oil changes and leaky faucets. Most of his visits had been to older ladies who plied him with sweet tea and jars of homemade jam and talked about the good old days while he replaced a fuse or unstopped the sink. And their houses had been quiet. Real quiet.

Rainy Jernagen stepped back, motioned him in, and Nate very cautiously entered a room that should have had flashing red lights and a *danger zone* sign.

Toys littered the living room like Christmas morning. An overturned cereal bowl flowed milk onto a coffee table. Next to a playpen crowding one wall, a green package belched out disposable diapers. Similarly, baby clothes were strewn, along with a couple of kids, on the couch and floor. In a word, the place was a wreck.

"The washer is back this way behind the kitchen. Watch your step. It's slippery."

More than slippery. Nate kicked his way through the living room and the kitchen area beyond, though the kitchen actually appeared much tidier than the rest, other than the slow seepage of water coming from somewhere beyond. The shine of liquid glistening on beige tile led them straight to the utility room.

"I turned the faucets off behind the washer when this first started, but a tubful still managed to pump out onto the floor." She hoisted the babies higher on her hip and spoke to a young boy sitting in the floor. "Joshua, get out of those suds."

"But they're pretty, Miss Rainy." The brown-haired boy with bright-blue eyes grinned up at her, extending a handful of bubbles. Light reflected off each droplet. "See the rainbows? There's always a rainbow, like you said. A rainbow behind the rain."

Miss Rainy smiled at the child. "Yes, there is. But right now, Mr. Del Rio needs in here to fix the washer. It's a little crowded for all of us." She was right about that. The space was no bigger than a small bathroom. "Can I get you to take the babies to the playpen while I show him around?"

"I'll take them, Miss Rainy." An older boy with a serious face and brown plastic glasses entered the room. Treading carefully, he came forward and took both babies, holding them against his slight chest. Another child appeared behind him. This one a girl with very blond hair and eyes the exact blue of the boy's, the one she'd called Joshua. How many children did this woman have, anyway? Six?

A heavy, smothery feeling pressed against his airway. Six kids?

Before he could dwell on that disturbing thought, a scream of sonic proportions rent the soap-fragrant air. He whipped around ready to protect and defend.

The little blond girl and the redhead were going at it.

"It's mine." Blondie tugged hard on a Barbie doll.

"It's mine. Will said so." To add emphasis to her demand, the redhead screamed bloody murder. "Miss Rainy."

About that time, Joshua decided to skate across the suds, and then slammed into the far wall next to a door that probably opened into the garage. He grabbed his big toe and set up a howl. Water sloshed as Rainy rushed forward and gathered him into her arms.

"Rainy!" Blondie screamed again.

"Rainy!" the redhead yelled.

Nate cast a glance at the garage exit and considered a fast escape.

Lord, I'm here to do a good thing. Can you help me out a little?

Rainy, her clothes now wet, somehow managed to take the doll from the fighting girls while snuggling Joshua against her side. The serious-looking boy stood in the doorway, a baby on each hip, taking in the chaos.

"Come on, Emma," the boy said to Blondie. "I'll make you some chocolate milk." So they went, slip-sliding out of the flooded room.

Four down, two to go.

Nate clunked his toolbox onto the washer and tried to ignore the chaos. Not an easy task, but one he'd learned to deal with as a boy. As an adult, he did everything possible to avoid this kind of madness. The Lord had a sense of humor sending him to this particular house.

"I apologize, Mr. Del Rio," Rainy said, shoving at the wads of hair that hung around her face like Spanish moss.

"Call me Nate. I'm not that much older than you." At thirty-one and the long-time patriarch of his family, he might feel seventy, but he wasn't.

"Okay, Nate. And I'm Rainy. Really, it's not usually this bad. I can't thank you enough for coming over. I tried to get a plumber, but being Saturday..." she shrugged, letting the obvious go unsaid. No one could get a plumber on the weekend.

"No problem." He removed his white Stetson and placed it

next to the toolbox. What was he supposed to say? That he loved wading in dirty soap suds and listening to kids scream and cry? Not likely.

Rainy stood with an arm around each of the remaining children—the rainbow boy and the redhead. Her look of embarrassment had him feeling sorry for her. All these kids and no man around to help. With this many, she'd never find another husband, he was sure of that. Who would willingly take on a boatload of kids?

After a minute, Rainy and the remaining pair left the room and he got to work. Wiggling the machine away from the wall wasn't easy. Even with all the water on the floor, a significant amount remained in the tub. This leftover liquid sloshed and gushed at regular intervals. In minutes, his boots were dark with moisture. No problem there. As a rancher, his boots were often dark with lots of things, the best of which was water.

On his haunches, he surveyed the back of the machine, where hoses and cords and metal parts twined together like a nest of water moccasins.

As he investigated each hose in turn, he once more felt a presence in the room. Pivoting on his heels, he discovered the two boys squatted beside him, attention glued to the back of the washer.

"A busted hose?" the oldest one asked, pushing up his glasses.

"Most likely."

"I coulda fixed it but Rainy wouldn't let me."

"That so?"

"Yeah. Maybe. If someone would show me."

Nate suppressed a smile. "What's your name?"

"Will. This here's my brother, Joshua." He yanked a thumb at the younger one. "He's nine. I'm eleven. You go to Miss Rainy's church?"

"I do, but it's a big church. I don't think we've met before."

"She's nice. Most of the time. She never hits us or anything, and we've been here for six months."

It occurred to Nate then that these were not Rainy's children. The kids called her Miss Rainy, not Mom, and according to Will they had not been here forever. But what was a young, single woman doing with all these kids?

* * * * *

Look for
HOME TO CROSSROADS RANCH
by Linda Goodnight,
on sale March 2009
only from Steeple Hill Love Inspired®,
available wherever books are sold.

Love Inspired

What do you do when Mr. Right doesn't want kids? Rainy Jernagen and her houseful of foster children won't let a little thing like that get in the way of bringing handyman Nate Del Rio home to them once and for all.

Look for

Home to Crossroads Ranch

by

Linda Goodnight

Available March wherever books are sold, including most bookstores, supermarkets, drugstores and discount stores.

www.SteepleHill.com

REQUEST YOUR FREE BOOKS!

2 FREE INSPIRATIONAL NOVELS
PLUS 2
FREE
MYSTERY GIFTS

YES! Please send me 2 FREE Love Inspired® novels and my 2 FREE mystery gifts (gifts are worth about $10). After receiving them, if I don't wish to receive any more books, I can return the shipping statement marked "cancel". If I don't cancel, I will receive 4 brand-new novels every month and be billed just $4.24 per book in the U.S. or $4.74 per book in Canada, plus 25¢ shipping and handling per book and applicable taxes, if any*. That's a savings of over 20% off the cover price! I understand that accepting the 2 free books and gifts places me under no obligation to buy anything. I can always return a shipment and cancel at any time. Even if I never buy another book, the two free books and gifts are mine to keep forever.

113 IDN ERXA 313 IDN ERWX

Name	(PLEASE PRINT)

Address	Apt. #

City	State/Prov.	Zip/Postal Code

Signature (if under 18, a parent or guardian must sign)

Order online at www.LoveInspiredBooks.com

Or mail to Steeple Hill Reader Service:

IN U.S.A.: P.O. Box 1867, Buffalo, NY 14240-1867
IN CANADA: P.O. Box 609, Fort Erie, Ontario L2A 5X3

Not valid to current subscribers of Love Inspired books.

Want to try two free books from another series?
Call 1-800-873-8635 or visit www.morefreebooks.com

* Terms and prices subject to change without notice. N.Y. residents add applicable sales tax. Canadian residents will be charged applicable provincial taxes and GST. Offer not valid in Quebec. This offer is limited to one order per household. All orders subject to approval. Credit or debit balances in a customer's account(s) may be offset by any other outstanding balance owed by or to the customer. Please allow 4 to 6 weeks for delivery. Offer available while quantities last.

Your Privacy: Steeple Hill Books is committed to protecting your privacy. Our Privacy Policy is available online at www.SteepleHill.com or upon request from the Reader Service. From time to time we make our lists of customers available to reputable third parties who may have a product or service of interest to you. If you would prefer we not share your name and address, please check here.

LIRFG08R

TITLES AVAILABLE NEXT MONTH

Available February 24, 2009

A SOLDIER FOR KEEPS by Jillian Hart
The McKaslin Clan

Handsome Army Ranger Pierce Granger knows he's found a
friend in Lexie Evans, the girl he rescued from a skiing accident.
Yet as their friendship grows, Lexie realizes she wants a forever
love, if Pierce is ready to be hers for keeps.

SOMEBODY'S HERO by Annie Jones

Finding a hero for her daughter wasn't what Charity O'Clare had
in mind when she moved to Mt. Knott, South Carolina, to sell
her late husband's cabin. Jason Burdett and his meddling family
may not have been in her plans, but there's no denying he's in
Charity's heart.

HOME TO CROSSROADS RANCH by Linda Goodnight

What do you do when Mr. Right doesn't want kids?
Rainy Jernagen and her houseful of foster children won't let
a little thing like that get in the way of bringing handyman
Nate Del Rio home to them once and for all.

A DROPPED STITCHES WEDDING by Janet Tronstad
Steeple Hill Café

Being the wedding planner *and* a bridesmaid means no time
for romance for Lizabett McDonald…until longtime crush
Rick Keifer steps in to help her make their friends' wedding
wishes come true. With their new faith and some careful plans
of Rick's own, this beautiful bridesmaid may just become a
blushing bride.

LICNMBPA0209